MW01139090

BOOK
boyfriend
when reality is better than fiction.

DAWN L. CHILETZ

Library of Congress Cataloging-in-Publication Data

Chiletz, Dawn L.
Book Boyfriend – 1st edition
ISBN-13: 978-1726836319

To the Will Coopers, Edward Cullens,
Christian Greys, and Penn Fitzgeralds
of the world.
I know you're out there.
We're waiting for you.

CHAPTER 1

Sepia with flecks of wheat.

If I were writing right now, those would be the exact words I'd use to describe the color of his eyes. I imagine opening my laptop and typing the words. His eyes—damn, I could get lost in them. Books are written about eyes like his. They really are the perfect shade of brown. Not at all boring and one-dimensional like mine. Deep brown pools of chocolate with peanut butter streaks of gold. Ooh, that's good. I wiggle my toes with excitement. Could this be the breakthrough I was hoping for? I try to remember the phrasing as I burn the fine lines under his lashes into my memory.

You'd think, under the circumstances, my mind would be otherwise occupied with more pressing matters. Say, for instance, the long fingers of his left hand, which are currently cupping my breast. The proximity of lips never tasted so close to my own. Or perhaps, the weight of his hard body pressed firmly against mine in the sand. Maybe even the dumbfounded expression on his face as he stares at me hoping for some kind of sign. It's as if, at this moment, any word from me could make or break his life.

I open my mouth and nothing comes out. That rarely ever happens. I'm known for always having something to say. But in between the crashing of waves against the shore and the rapid pulsating of my heart in my chest, I can't seem to find the words to express myself.

I think I'm starting to feel . . . pain. The jarred feeling in my bones confirms it. Sand isn't soft like people think it is. It's tiny little pieces of shells, mineral deposits, and granular rock. Most people see the luxurious ripples of sand, watch their feet sink into it like silk, and assume it's a soft material, but when your head hits it at fifty miles an hour, you're forced to consider that sand is not a soft, fluffy pillow. It's a freight train of steel crushed into pebbles.

It's a good analogy. I really am a walking encyclopedia. I should probably spend less time with my face buried in books. Maybe I wouldn't be in this precarious situation if I paid more attention to the world around me. Looking up into those eyes once more, I sigh. Who am I kidding? This is the most action I've had in forever. I should probably try to enjoy it.

It amazes me how fast the human mind works. I've had all these thoughts in a matter of seconds, although it feels like a lot longer. Glancing down at my chest, I watch his fingers pulse along the material of my pink bathing suit before he firmly palms my right tit as if to steady himself. I say the first thing that comes into my mind when I sense he's about to panic.

"You could've at least bought me dinner before you copped a feel."

I almost regret making a joke when he feverishly moves

his eyes from mine to the location of his fingers. He cringes as his lips open and words escape him. His hands move to the sand. He lifts himself off me like he's doing a push-up and moves to sit at my side.

"I'm just kidding," I say through a half-smile although I am a little hungry. As I rise up on my elbows, I moan lightly when my brain rattles against my skull.

"I'm so sorry! Oh fuck, are you okay?" he asks.

He said fuck. Now that his muscled thighs are directly in front of me, I'm kind of wishing I were actually underneath him for that reason.

He soars up off the ground effortlessly, as if he's floating, and reaches out for my arms to help me sit up. I wave them away.

How quickly the tides have turned. Another beach analogy. Damn, I have issues.

Not more than a couple of minutes ago, I was sitting in my lounge chair near the ocean watching bikini babes strut their perfect bodies along the shore. I remember I'd started to feel inadequate. The self-loathing kicked in as I fell into body comparison mode and began to question my life choices. Especially the bagel I had for breakfast and the slice of pizza for lunch. Then I realized that coming to the ocean for book ideas was a monumental mistake. As soon as I made the decision to forget this whole inspiration vacation and go back home, I immediately jumped up and got knocked on my ass by the complete and total hottie now standing desperately concerned in front of me.

"Do you need a doctor?" His hands rush through his wavy, dark hair before he reaches out to me again and pulls back. He's a nervous wreck.

"I'm fine. Really. Just give me a second." Shaking my head to get my bearings, the loose sand from my short black hair scatters over my shoulders.

He crouches down next to me. "This is totally my fault. I was running along the beach and I swear I heard someone call my name. I only turned my head for a second. I didn't even see you."

I blink a few times and try to see past the rays of light shining behind him. I can't see his face, but I can most definitely hear laughter all around me. Super. I just love drawing attention to myself in the worst way possible. My sole focus becomes trying not to look as dumb as I feel. Pushing up from the ground, I almost lose my balance. One of his hands grabs my arm and the other grips my waist.

"Whoa there. Are you really okay?"

I briefly stare at his hand on my hip before stepping out of his reach and brushing the sand from my arms. "I'm really okay."

Turning my head left and right to the lingering onlookers, I shout, "Show's over, folks, but tips are welcome."

He snickers and I cock my head to the side, raising my palm over my eyes to get a better look at his face in the sun. I know my mouth gapes, but I can't help it. Fuck me twice and call me stupid. I couldn't have picked a better looking guy to plow into me if I tried.

He's tall and built. No wonder it felt like I got hit by a brick. He is one. A brick house with a naked, inviting chest and arm muscles like strong, deep-rooted trees that make you want to climb them. I unconsciously lick my lips as I take in his stomach muscles. Those waves are better than the ones on the beach.

He clears his throat and I glance up at his face in time to see he's caught me ogling him. I silently berate myself for drooling over him and quickly throw on my ratted Fall Out Boy T-shirt. I must have hit my head harder than I thought. I usually don't even bother looking at the pretty boys. I bend down to pick up my laptop, now covered in sand.

"Is your computer okay?"

I flip it open and shake it out. "Yeah, I'm sure it's fine. It's just a little dirt. This baby has withstood three cups of coffee and two diet cokes. I'm sure a little sand is refreshing for him."

"Him?"

"I'd like to think it's a man. I mean, I have my hands all over him all day long and he never complains, so . . ."

He laughs as he bends down to fold my chair. "Let me get that for you."

I touch his arm and stop him mid reach. "It's fine. I'm fine. You're off the hook. You can go back to your jog or whatever. Maybe find that person who called your name."

"Fisher," he says.

"Me? No. Do I look like I fish?"

He smirks. "That's my name. Well, my last name. Patrick Fisher. But everyone calls me Fisher."

"Oh. Okay. Cool. Thanks for sharing."

I shake out my towel and stuff it into my bag along with my bottle of sunscreen and my laptop. Just as I lift the bag from the ground, he grabs it from me and tosses it on his shoulder.

"Hey, what's your deal?" I place my hands on my hips.

"Let me carry your things. It's the least I can do for all the trouble I caused."

"I'm right here," I say, motioning to the hotel just beyond the swimming pool. "I'm going back to my room. It's not necessary."

He sighs. "I feel terrible for knocking you over. You were a little wobbly and I'd feel better if I could just walk you to the hotel."

"You're not the first guy who's knocked my off my feet. I'm fine. Really." I reach out for my bag and he steps back.

Pausing to stare at him for a moment, I shake my head and bend down to grab my folded chair. He rushes in and takes it before my hand is halfway there.

"What am I supposed to carry?" I ask as I slip on my flip-flops.

"Someone as beautiful as you should never have to lift a thing."

My eyebrows rise in amusement and I snort. "There are no fish in this sea, Fisher. You should take your rod and move on to bigger oceans."

"My rod?" He laughs. "Wow, I guess that sounded like a pick-up line, didn't it?" He cringes humorously.

I shrug. "I call 'em like I see 'em."

"I like that. And it may have sounded like a line, but I meant it. You really are gorgeous." He squints and licks his lips cautiously. "I'm sure men tell you that all the time."

Wrinkling my nose, I decide to let him believe that's true. I don't think now is the time to pour out my troubled dating life to a complete stranger. He doesn't seem like a player. He's too nervously awkward. I think. What do I know? I haven't been on a date in like . . . crap. Five years? My reality reminds me I need to move. The sooner I get off the beach, the sooner I can get my ass back to my room to change my flight home.

Home. The word sounds like heaven right now. I imagine my soft comforter and my own perfect bed. I want to go home and sleep for a week.

He follows closely behind as I silently walk past the pool to the hotel entrance. Turning to face him, I hold out my hand for him to give me my bag. He places his hand inside mine instead, shaking it. Damn, he has big hands.

"I didn't get your name."

"That's because I didn't tell you," I reply.

I attempt to take my hand back, but he won't let go. He raises an eyebrow at me and smiles a crooked smile that almost makes me lose my will to breathe. Holy fucktits. He's not just hot, he's beautiful. Like a tanned god. I stammer now because I realize I need to get away from him before my wet panties drip down my leg. "Greer. Greer Hanson." Shit. I just gave him my real name. I usually give my author name to strangers.

"I wish we had met under better circumstances, Greer, and again, I apologize for running you down."

He releases my hand and slides my bag down his arm. I nod and stare at the ground awkwardly, wondering when I can run away without looking like I'm running.

"I'd be happy to carry this back to your room for you, if you'd like."

I shoot him my best Britney Spears crazy face and he chuckles.

"I did it again, didn't I?" The irony of his words and my thoughts has me singing, "Oops, I Did It Again" in my head.

"That's not what I meant. I just . . . What I mean is . . ."

I shift uncomfortably from foot to foot as he attempts to clarify. I slip the straps of my bag over my shoulder. This is kind of weird. Even for me.

His hand rushes through his hair once more. "Could I buy you a drink?" he asks.

Oh jeez. He *really* feels bad. I place my hand on my heart. "No. Thank you. Oh my gosh. It was an accident. You don't owe me anything. Please stop feeling like you do. It was nice to meet you and thank you, but I have a lot of work to do and I need to go."

He opens his mouth and closes it abruptly before smiling and nodding. I take the opportunity and speed walk away from him. I slowly glance over my shoulder to see he's still watching me. He raises his hand to wave and I face forward, itching my chin on my shoulder like I wasn't intentionally turning to him. I finish my walk like it's an Olympic event and I'm determined to win first place. Once I've made my way through the lobby and I'm safely inside the closed elevator, I start to laugh. What the hell was that? Weird shit happens to me all the time, but this is one for the books.

CHAPTER 2

"**Y**ou can't come home. You owe me a book and so help me God you're going to at *least* give me an outline."

I wish I hadn't answered my phone when I returned to my room. She might be my publisher, but she was my best friend first. I'm certain it comes as no surprise to her when I speak my mind. "Fuck it, Luna. It's not going to happen."

Yes, her name is Luna. Luna Lord. And no, she's not a porn star, she just has the name of one.

"It is going to happen. You're three months late on a deadline I pushed back a year already. Do you know how far I've bent for you?" she asks.

"Like a gymnast who wants to be fucked with her head by her ass?"

"Farther than that," she responds.

"I know." I sigh as I toss my beach bag onto the couch and wander over to my oceanfront balcony. "I thought coming here would help, but it didn't. I think we just need to face the fact that not only did Oliver get the house in the divorce, but he also got my mojo."

"No, he did not. That piece of shit, cheating scumbag does not get to take your career along with his old ass whore and half your income."

Opening the doors, the cool breeze calms my flaming skin. I'm either stressed or burned. It's hard to tell right now.

"I know it was painful for you. I know he hurt you. But you're only thirty-one. You're young, and single, and in prime position to have this fall's new blockbuster book. I know you've got it in you. You're not a bestselling author for nothing. You have skills. You write like no one I've ever seen. You can do this. You just need a story. Give me a line. Even a title. One fricking small idea and we'll run with it!"

"I know you're trying to help and I'm sorry I've been such a slug all these months. I don't know why I thought traveling to Florida would somehow make me write. There are beaches in California and I can't write there either."

"You can write. Stop saying you can't. How many times do I have to tell you about the law of attraction? Stop putting all those negative thoughts out into the world. Be positive. Positive attracts positive."

"Yeah, yeah," I say, rolling my eyes. I drop my phone to the table and press the speakerphone button so I can change out of my bathing suit.

"Am I on speakerphone? Dammit, I hate that!" she shouts.

"I know, but I'm full of sand and I need to shower. I can't stand the way I feel right now." I carry the phone with me to the bathroom and place it on the sink while I run the water.

"You hate sand. I thought you checked out a beach chair

for that reason."

"I did, but, well, some guy ran me down and I ended up under him. It's everywhere." I step into the shower and immediately turn down the water temperature. Now I *know* I got burned. Crap.

"I'm sorry, what? You were under a guy? Why am I just hearing this now?"

"It's not a big deal."

"You anywhere near a guy is a big deal."

"Shut your pie hole!" I half shout, half laugh. She's right, though. Ever since I caught my now ex cheating, I've barely held a conversation with another man, much less wanted to date one. I avoid them like the plague. I see all of them as potential liars now. I can't help it.

"Tell me what happened. I want all the details. Was he cute?"

"No."

"Aww, he was fugly?" she asks.

"No."

"Well, what was he then?"

I can tell she's flustered.

"Let's just say if Chris Hemsworth had a dark-haired brother, it would have been him."

"He does have a brother. Two of them. Liam and Luke."

"No, not Liam, and he was way taller than Luke. A twin then; a dark-haired replica." How in the hell does sand reach every fricking little crevice?

"I thought you said he wasn't cute."

"He wasn't cute. He was drop dead fucking hotter than fuck."

I hear her squeal, as I turn off the water and step out of

the shower. Just as I'm about to lather on some lotion, there's a knock at my door. "Hold on, Luna. Someone's at the door."

"Take me with you. We're not done talking."

I throw on the hotel robe and rush to the peephole. I can see the uniform. It looks like someone who works here. "Can I help you?"

He turns and he's holding a vase of at least two dozen roses. "I have a delivery for Greer Hanson, room six-fourteen."

"What did he say? A delivery?" Luna shouts from the table.

"Shh. Hold on a second."

"No problem, miss. Take your time."

"No, not you," I say to the door.

"Not me what?" Luna asks.

I open the door quickly to avoid any more confusion. Shocked isn't a strong enough word to describe my reaction. "For me? Are you sure?"

"You're Greer, right?"

I nod and he smiles. He has me sign a little card before I take them. They're beautiful and fragrant. Each rose is just as perfect as the one next to it. I've never ever received flowers like this. It almost makes me blush. I lift a finger to the delivery man. "Hold on a sec." I rush to find my purse and he stops me.

"Oh no, miss. My tip was covered. Have a great day!"

I close the door behind him and carry the flowers to the table. "Did you do this?" I ask into the air, directing my question to Luna.

"Do what? What did you get?"

"The most beautiful flowers I've ever seen."

"Hell, no. You want flowers from me, write me a damn

book. Is there a card?"

I use the back arm of my robe to wipe the trickle of water from my wet hair out of my eye. Then I reach for the card. "Who would send me flowers?" I ask. "It was you, don't lie."

"I swear it wasn't. Open it! Read it out loud."

Tearing open the paper a little too anxiously, I read, "Greer, I know we just met and this is crazy, but I'd love to see you again. Dinner maybe? Fisher." I slump down into the chair by the table and re-read the card again. It's cute in a dorky sort of way. He left his number. What the actual fuck?

"Fisher? Who the hell is Fisher?"

"The guy who knocked me down. He must really have a guilty conscience."

"Are you for real? Did he leave his number?"

"Yes."

"Call him!"

"No. No way."

"So help me God, Greer. You need to call Chris Hemsworth's twin! Do it!"

"No, I can't!"

"Why? Why can't you?" she asks.

"Because."

"Give me his number then. I'd call a guy who looked like Chris Hemsworth's left *nostril*."

I chuckle and toss the card on the table. I pick up the phone and go back into the bathroom. Dropping my robe, I start applying lotion to my skin. Why in the world would he send me flowers? How did he get my room number? Should I be flattered or frightened? I mean, he did make my head spin, but maybe that was because I have a brain injury.

"Hello? Are you there?" Luna asks.

"Yeah, sorry."

"I know what's going on. I want you to listen to me. Okay? You are a beautiful, strong, independent, talented woman who has had what seems to be a crap load of bad luck lately. But the truth is, Oliver did you a favor when he cheated. He gave you the reason you needed to leave a shitty marriage and find someone who appreciates the wonderful, intelligent person you are. You're on vacation. Go have a little fun with a hot stranger you'll never see again. Let him take you to a free dinner. Maybe let him make you cum. Have fun. You deserve it. Go live your life. Stop sitting on the sidelines inventing lives for fictional characters and make one for yourself!"

"Let him make me cum? Jesus, Luna. I'm not that girl. I've only ever been with Ollie. I'm not going to fuck some strange guy and come home with a disease."

"Is that all you heard? Who said fuck him? I said, let him make you cum. You don't need to fuck him for that!"

"This is ridiculous!" I bury my face in my arms and lean against the bathroom door.

"Call him! Call him! Call him!"

She's chanting and at first it pisses me off. But then, it makes me laugh. Maybe she's right. I am hungry. It's a free dinner. I'll reschedule my trip home for the morning, have dinner with a good-looking stranger, and then head home to focus on getting my life put back together. What do I have to lose?

She's still chanting. I consider just hanging up on her, but I say "Fine!" first. Pressing end call, I slip a light blue V-neck T-shirt over my head and walk back out into the living area. I start and stop dialing ten times before I'm finally able to call him. I use the hotel phone. There's no way he's getting my cell phone number.

"Hello?"

"Hi, umm, Patrick? I mean, Fisher? Yeah, you didn't need to send me flowers. I mean, they're really beautiful and all, but it wasn't necessary."

"I know they weren't necessary, but I really wanted to. Do you believe in fate, Greer?"

I can hear him smiling when he speaks. I can tell. I roll my eyes at myself for feeling giddy.

"Oh, shit, you're not one of those people, are you?" I ask.

"I am. I think there's a reason I ran into you. I haven't been able to get you out of my mind since."

"Maybe you hit your head, too."

"Did you hit your head?" he asks, suddenly worried.

"I'm fine."

"You could have a concussion. Now you have to let me see you. I need to make sure your eyes are fully dilated."

I laugh. "Do you run over people on purpose? Is this your MO?"

"Have dinner with me."

"No."

"Have dinner with me."

"I said no." I laugh.

"Have dinner with me." His voice is deeper this time. It's sexy even through the phone. I pause.

"Please?"

"Fine. Gosh. Then you can see I'm not hurt and you can move on to the next girl on the beach."

"I'm going to ignore all the other stuff and focus on the fine. How about the steakhouse in your hotel in an hour?"

"No. Too fancy." I pause and glance out my window.

"How about the taco truck by the beach in thirty minutes?"

"Really?" He almost sounds excited.

"I like tacos."

"I'll see you in thirty minutes and you can have all the tacos you want."

"Okay, well, bring money, because I'm not one of those girls who get salad. I'm hungry."

He laughs. "I like hungry girls. I'll bring my wad. I mean . . ."

"Classy," I reply. "See you then." I hang up without giving him a chance to explain. I know what he meant, but I have to admit, there's a part of me that hopes he has a wad . . . in his pants, and I'll get to see it.

I always wanted to have a one-night stand. Maybe it's time I become one of the girls I only write about. Oh, who am I kidding? Sleeping with one guy in college and marrying him years later does not a sexual dynamo make. I do write sexy stories, though. No one would ever know I'd only been with one guy. Good thing I kept my maiden name and Oliver isn't allowed to disclose our marriage or anything else about me. At least I got my privacy in the divorce.

I guess I'm lucky I have such a vivid imagination. It keeps me busy on lonely nights. It's a bonus that authors are allowed to watch porn for "research" purposes. Maybe I should think of this dinner as research. I should get *something* out of this trip.

I dry my hair and find I don't need much makeup. I apply a little powder to my red face in an attempt to look like I'm not a fire breathing dragon and a little gloss to my lips. Why should I care what I look like? It's just tacos with a stranger. What could possibly go wrong?

CHAPTER 3

I'm ten minutes early. It's another issue of mine to add to my growing list. I hate being late, so I'm always too punctual. I'm the girl who shows up first at a party. Fashionably late? Not me. I can't do it. Luna usually tells me a party starts later than it really does so I'm not the first one there. She thinks I should make a grand entrance. I don't do anything grand. I usually show up, have a drink, smile for pictures, and then I'm ready to go home and take off my bra. Why do women have to wear them anyway? It's not fair.

Tugging at the strap on my shoulder, I attempt to reposition it so it's not on a burn line. Having to wear a bra when you have a sunburn is torturous. I walk toward the truck and skim the menu. If I weren't craving tacos, I would've probably just stayed in my room. A small part of me wants to grab three or four, ooh and some chips and guacamole, go back to my room, turn on the TV, stuff my face, and go to sleep.

I bite my bottom lip and step into the line. Maybe he'll be late or better yet, maybe he won't show. My eyes shuffle left and right as I decide that binge eating alone sounds way better than making small talk.

"What can I get you, darlin'?" The taco truck man smiles as he wipes his hands on a rag.

"Which would you recommend, the steak or chicken?"

"They're both good."

"I'd recommend two of each," a voice smolders over my shoulder.

I turn to see Fisher standing behind me smiling. His hair is coiffed in perfection and he looks like he stepped out of a page in a magazine. I'm caught off guard by both his presence and his voice.

I do a double take and attempt to refocus on the menu.

"Two of each?" the food truck cashier asks.

"Umm, two steak, one chicken," I reply.

"Make that four steak and three chicken," Fisher replies. He leans in, placing his lips near my ear as he steps closer behind me. "What would you like to drink?" he whispers seductively.

Okay, it probably wasn't a seductive question, but his warm breath on my ear, his proximity, and the smell of his skin force an eruption of goose bumps on my arms. He could have asked me if I had toe jam and it would have sounded hot.

I eye the board for drink options.

"We have killer margaritas," truck guy says as he points toward a picture by the open window.

Fisher leans forward, turning his head to see my face. "Sound good?"

I nod.

He stands next to me, his shoulder touching mine. "Two of those too, please."

He reaches into his wallet and I start to reach into my shorts for cash out of habit. When I was with Ollie, I usually paid.

"Oh no, you don't," he says, placing his hand over mine. "This is my treat, remember?"

I nod again, feeling awkward. "Chips and guacamole too," I shout out. What the hell. How often do guys buy me dinner?

Fisher smiles as the taco truck driver looks at him. "She can have anything she wants."

I suddenly feel confident. I haven't had a guy be this nice to me in forever. "Anything?" I question, turning to face him.

His dark eyes meet mine and his smile fades. "Anything."

Oh shit. Spinning around to face forward, I say, "Chips and guac then."

Could I really have *anything* with him? Like, if I asked him to climb back on top of me and grind his hips into me, would he do it? I shush my inner dialogue. Why am I acting this way? Luna. It's all her fault. She put stupid ideas in my head. I'm going to eat until I'm stuffed and go back to my room. That's it. This is an apology dinner. Nothing more.

"Thank you," I say, turning to face him. "You didn't have to do this."

"I know that. I wanted to. Plus, it is Taco Tuesday after all."

I grin. Now he's speaking my language.

Our margaritas are the first thing ready. He hands me mine and we both take a sip at the same time. "Yum," I say as my eyes roll back in my head.

"He wasn't kidding."

The taco man hands Fisher all the food in a box and Fisher motions toward a picnic table nearby.

I climb into my seat and refrain from greedily grabbing my food from him. It smells so good. He divvies up the tacos and pushes the chips and guac my way.

"You can have some. I'll share," I tell him.

I hand him a fully loaded chip and he stuffs it into his mouth in one bite.

We start eating and it's gloriously quiet. The waves on the beach and our mutual moans of approval as we bask in food glory are the only background noise. As I open my second taco he breaks the silence.

"What brings you to the Keys?" he asks.

"Maybe I live here."

"In a hotel? I think not."

"What if I'm really homeless but I saved up enough money for one night in a nice place?"

"Most homeless people don't have mani-pedis with red nail polish."

I gaze down at my hand. "What if I won an all-inclusive stay in a contest?"

"Did that contest include a laptop?"

"Hmm . . . What if my laptop was the only possession I had left?"

"That and a Fall Out Boy concert T-shirt from last year's tour?" he asks as he reaches over and loads a chip with a guacamole and hands it to me.

He's very observant. I take the chip and stuff it into my mouth in one bite just like he did. He laughs.

When I've almost finished chewing I cover my mouth slightly with my hand and say, "Maybe I'm newly homeless or found the shirt in a dumpster."

"You don't like personal questions, do you?"

I choose to ignore the question because he figured me out too quickly. "What brings *you* to the Keys?" I ask, diverting the attention.

"Work. I travel a lot. I rarely get me time, but this trip was different. I actually have a day all to myself for once."

The next obvious question would be what do you do? But I don't want to get too personal. I'm leaving tomorrow and I'll never see him again, so why should I care?

He stops eating and stares at me for a moment. I think he's waiting for me to ask him, but I don't. I take a giant bite of my taco and watch half of it drip out the other side.

"You're different."

I sigh as I open my taco and reload it with my fingers. I'm not letting any of this deliciousness go to waste. "You mean a mess?"

"No, not at all. You seem to know exactly who you are. It's very appealing. You're not like other girls."

Motioning to my body, I reply, "This is all woman, Fisher. What you see is what you get."

"I like what I see and I'll take any of it I can get."

Oh boy. He's a flirt and a half. I decide to let it slide. I take another bite before I tuck a loose strand of hair behind my ear. He chuckles lightly, covering his mouth.

"What?" I ask, concerned.

He points to my head. I grab a napkin and wipe my lips. Crap. I probably have taco juice running down my face.

"No. There," he says, pointing again.

I wipe my cheeks, then my nose as he keeps laughing and I get it wrong.

"For fuck's sake, where?" I ask.

He reaches his hand across the table and pulls a small piece of tomato from my hair by my ear.

He holds it in his palm for me to see.

"Hey. That's mine. Get your own. I was saving that for later." I place it back on my ear and refocus on my taco.

"My God, you're beautiful."

I stop mid bite and stare at him. He's making serious direct eye contact.

Placing my taco on the table, I take a long drink from my margarita in an effort to think what I want to say. I wipe my hands on a napkin and briefly roll my tongue around my teeth to dislocate any loose pieces of meat or cheese before I speak. Then, I let it fly.

"What's the plan here?" I ask. "You see a woman on the beach who's obviously alone. You run her down, take her to dinner, woo her with your charm, and then what? Bed her and steal her cash while she sleeps?"

"Am I wooing you?"

"That sounds like an admission."

He sighs. "First of all, if I'd scoped you out and wanted to meet you, I wouldn't have knocked you over. I'm not that kind of guy. I might have tripped in front of you or hell, just stopped and introduced myself. Secondly, I didn't know you were alone, but I hoped you were single when I didn't see a wedding ring. Third, I don't think I'm charming in the least, but I'm trying to be. I'm not sure it's doing me any favors. Fourth, I don't need any money. I have cash of my own."

"You forgot the bed her part."

He leans forward, placing his elbows on the table. "I'd like to leave that option open."

I deadpan stare. Is he serious? What the ever loving fuck?

I don't know what to say to that. We stare at each other forever before his lip slowly curls on the side and he starts to laugh.

"All I want is tacos and some conversation on a gorgeous night on the beach. I rarely have time to enjoy myself and you fascinate me. You make having a good night easy. There's no pretense here. No expectations. No hidden agenda. Okay?"

He seems legit. I almost feel bad for assuming anything. "That's good to know. Because I'm not *that* kind of girl and if you think anything is going to happen you're going to be disappointed."

"Fair enough." He slaps his palms together and motions to my almost empty cup. "How about another drink?"

"Only if I can pay this time."

"Nope," he says as he stands. "I'm not *that* kind of guy."

I can't help but smile. That was a good comeback. No, a great one. I make a mental note of it. As he steps into line at the taco truck, I watch him. Why in the world is this man talking to me? I'm not his type, am I? I glance down at the tattoo on my thigh and then at the one on my arm. I don't see a single tattoo on his body. I lift my hand and touch the four piercings in my ear. I bet he's never pierced anything.

At least three or four girls stare at him as they walk past. He doesn't seem to notice. Is he for real?

Crumpling wrappers, I start cleaning up the table. I need to focus on something other than him. I walk over to the trash can to throw everything away then stop to admire the sun as it starts to set in the horizon. It's breathtaking.

His arm stretches out around me with my new margarita and I take it from him. "Thank you. And I'm sorry if I seem paranoid. I have issues with trust."

His eyes darken as he gazes down into my eyes. "Trust

has to be earned. I don't trust many people either."

"Oh really?" I ask, taking a sip from my drink. "Who do you trust?"

He ponders my question for a moment as he takes a drink and faces the setting sun. "I trust my mom, my younger brother, my best friend Chloe, and . . . my dog."

"That's a good list," I say with a smile.

"What about you?" he asks, leaning on a rail. "Who do you trust?"

I shrug my shoulders and let minutes of silence pass us by.

"How many of those margaritas will it take to get you to tell me about yourself?"

I shrug again.

"How about a walk on the beach?"

I wrinkle my nose. "I'm not a fan of sand."

"Oh, come on. It's just your toes. I promise I won't let you get knocked over by anyone. I'll protect you from dirt and non-observant runners. I'll even carry you if you'd like."

I snicker as he starts to walk around the railing and motions with his head for me to follow him. "Come on, Greer. Take a chance."

I sing "Take a Chance on Me" by ABBA in my head as I watch him. My apprehension seems to be fleeting. Fisher is so carefree and light, like nothing bothers him. He's a positivity magnet. He also seems to be daring me by the "take a chance" comment. Greer Hanson might be nervous, but Macy Greer, author extraordinaire, would never shy away from a dare. I summon her silently and laugh at myself.

Maybe this sunburn is poisoning my usually impeccable judgement. Or maybe the alcohol I rarely drink is making me more carefree. For once, I don't think. I simply slide off my flip-flops and follow him. Part of me feels that tonight, I might just follow him anywhere.

CHAPTER 4

We walk in silence. It's . . . nice. I like the quiet. I especially like not having to answer questions. The cool breeze feels amazing on my skin. The waves wash over my toes, making me forget we're in sand at all. Every once in a while I bend over to pick up a sea shell. He starts pointing them out to me after he notices my fascination with them. I begin collecting them and when my cup-less hand gets full, he takes them from me and places them in his pocket.

After I finish my drink, he takes my empty cup from me and runs them to the trash can nearby. He makes jogging on the beach look effortless. I can barely walk in deep sand without stumbling. "Having fun?" he asks as he returns to me.

"Yeah. I think I am."

"Good. So, can I hold your hand?" he asks, reaching out to me and looking adorably unsure.

I shrug as I place my hand in his and he smiles like he won a prize. It makes me feel good. Better than I've felt in a long time. His hand wrapped around mine doesn't suck either.

I haven't held a man's hand in ages. I forgot how good it feels. I imagine a crack forming in the wall I've built around myself. It slowly crumbles more and more the longer we walk.

He limits his questions to things like, "How about this shell?" or "Have you ever seen anything like it?" It's comforting. Those are questions I can and want to answer.

It's getting darker by the minute. I can almost make out his face by the light from the hotels nearby, but he has to face me in a certain direction and I really have to focus to see him. I'm not sure how far we've walked, but it's got to be getting late. I could check my phone for the time, but it's tucked inside my bra and I don't want to reach for it. I turn and gaze back to see just how far we are from the hotel. I can't tell.

"Do you need to go?" he asks.

"Yeah. I probably should. I have a morning flight home tomorrow and I still need to pack."

"Where's home?"

"California."

He nods. Is that sadness I see? My heart flutters in my chest. I think I feel it too.

He squeezes my hand as we turn. Is it just me or are we both walking slower? He doesn't say another word for several minutes. I shiver as a new gust of air hits my warm skin.

"Are you cold?"

"I'm okay. I got a little too much sun today." I wrap my free arm around myself.

"I'm a furnace. I'd be okay, if you wanted to lean against me while we walk. I did say I'd protect you. That means protection from wind as well."

I stop abruptly and he takes a step forward before he notices, never letting go of my hand. I glance down at our hands outstretched in front of us and it looks . . . right. I suddenly feel like I've known him forever and that my hand belongs in his.

"What is it?" he asks, facing me.

"I don't know. I . . . I don't want this night to end."

He gazes out at the line of hotels in the distance then his eyes meet mine. He moves in a little closer to me and the gap between us shrinks. When I don't react, he inches forward slightly more. Then more. I smile. "Testing the waters?"

"I don't want to push my luck."

I sigh. "There's only room for one more step between us and I haven't backed away yet. That should be a sign."

He lifts his hand and brushes the hair away from my face. He holds out the piece of tomato in his hand. "Did you still want this?"

I laugh. "Oh my God. Have I had that in my hair the entire time? Why didn't you say anything?"

"Because you seem to be extremely fond of tomatoes?"

He poses it like a question. I take it from his hand and pop it in my mouth. "Still yummy."

He laughs hardily and I have to steady myself. It affects me to my core.

"That's one lucky tomato."

"Huh?" I question.

"I'd give anything to be in your mouth."

I swallow hard as he lessens the little space between us and his face inches closer to mine. Oh shit. He wants to be in my mouth. Does he mean his tongue? His finger? His dick? I wonder what his dick would taste like. Oh hell. Am I really considering that as an option? Do I want this? Him?

His lips are almost touching mine. I quickly run my tongue over my mouth. That's what I'm supposed to do, right?

That's what girls do in my stories. No one likes a dry lip. Oh damn, this is taking forever. This kiss scene would be exactly how I'd write it in my books, slow and building. But living it versus writing it is torture. It's taking too long. Kiss me already. Please.

When his lips finally touch mine I think I see fireworks behind my eyelids. Oh dear Lord in heaven, have mercy on my soul. Is this what I've been missing? Do all men other than Oliver kiss this way or is he a professional? What if he is a professional? What if he's a male hooker? Oh shit. I don't care. I want that tongue.

I open my mouth and slide my tongue against his. He pulls me closer to his chest and I feel my entire body relax into him. His hand sifts through my hair and he tugs on it lightly to bend my head back. His mouth leaves mine and moves to my neck. He plants soft kisses from my ear to my collarbone and then back up again before his lips meet mine once more.

I don't know how long we stand with our toes in the water making out. It must be a while, because a wave almost knocks us to the ground. As we stumble, we laugh. The water crashes again, higher this time, and hits my shorts. As if I weren't wet enough.

"Shit!" I scream.

"Don't worry, my lady! I'll save you."

I don't have time to do anything other than gasp as he lifts me into his arms and starts to run us away from the water.

"Fisher!" I want to protest his carrying me, but I laugh instead. He runs me away from the shore, then back toward the water, teasing me as waves hit him in the knees.

He does this repeatedly until I'm laughing so hard, I can't catch my breath. A wave hits him at the waist and he stops in the water. I loosen myself from his grip until I'm in the water too. The waves soak us both, but I don't care.

"You're getting wet," he says, running his fingers through his hair.

"I was wet the moment I saw you."

He grips his hair in his hands and sighs before smiling down at me. "You can't say things like that to a man. It does things to me I can't control."

I blink my eyes repeatedly. "I think I'd like to *see* what it's doing to you."

His eyebrows lift and he gives me a gaze I could only describe as smoldering. He takes my hand and places it on his wet shorts. I feel the bulge in his pants and I do what any sane woman would do. I grab ahold.

"Fuck," he whispers.

"No, but I wouldn't be against letting you feel the inside of my mouth."

"It's a beautiful mouth. But there are other lips I'd like to taste as well. It's only fair."

Oh damn. He's good. Am I really about to do this? Yes. Yes, I am.

I glance back and forth along the beach. There's no one in sight. I start to unzip his shorts as another wave crashes against us. I reach my hand inside and move the material away to reach him.

He's hard and thick. I swallow hard. What's gotten into me? I run my fingers over his length as he slowly trails his fingers up my thigh and under the material of my short shorts. His middle finger finds me immediately and he plunges it inside me. I moan. The water continues to crash against us as we stroke each other purposefully. His mouth crashes against mine and I lift my leg slightly, holding on to him for balance. He doesn't disappoint. It doesn't take long for my toes to curl as the waves of the ocean combine with my waves of orgasm. I increase my grip as well as my stride until I feel the warmth of his cum in my hand.

It's a brief feeling. The water quickly rushes it away, but it's enough to make me feel accomplished. He zips his zipper and touches my cheek with his palm.

He kisses me deeply and pulls me tightly to him. Placing my arms around his neck, he lifts me up until I'm straddling him.

He walks us out of the water and places me on the ground.

"Stay with me tonight?" he asks.

I shake my head. "That's an amazing offer, but . . ."

"But?"

"I can't." I close my eyes. What in the world did I just do? This isn't me. Greer Hanson doesn't fondle strangers on the beach. It was definitely liquid courage. The effects of the margaritas begin to slide away.

He leans in closer to me. "But I'm not done with you."

"Oh God, Fisher . . . Patrick. *That* was amazing. But I'm leaving tomorrow and we'll probably never see each other again. Maybe we should just let this be what it was and not . . . what did you say before? Push our luck?"

He nods reluctantly. "The little I know about you tells me that pleading will get me nowhere."

"You're a smart man."

"But what if I want to see you again?"

Ugh. Walking away from him, I ponder telling him what a hot mess I am and how he should run away from me.

I turn and notice he hasn't kept walking with me. He's still where I left him staring at me. I feel bad and walk back toward him. "I'm a mess, okay?" I shout over the sound of the waves. "I just went through an ugly divorce. My career is in shambles and I don't even know who I am right now. Trust me when I say you'd be better off remembering me this way."

"What way is that?" he asks. "Like this hot chick who played me?"

I laugh.

"You think that's funny, huh?" he says as he treads toward me.

"I think the fact *you* think I'm hot is funny. And me, playing anyone, isn't even remotely close to the truth. I don't know how to play anything, Fisher. And if you knew me, you'd know just how accurate that is."

"Let me get to know you then. At least give me your number."

He's not going to let this go. "Okay. That's doable."

He smiles as if he's won. He's everything I'd ever write a man to be. But men like him don't really exist. If I got to know him, I'd probably discover he really is a male prostitute. Or maybe he just escaped from prison. Or he has a wife and three kids at home. Oh damn, I hope not. I decide what I'm going to do as we walk back to the hotel. Some things are best left as perfect short stories with perfect endings. This is one of them.

I'm going to give him a number. Little does he know, it just won't be mine.

CHAPTER 5

Six months later

I sip my coffee and curl my legs under me as I stare out the window of Luna's office. I'm early as usual, but her secretary, Brenna, let me in. I noticed she had my new release folded open on her desk as she unlocked Luna's door. I asked her if she'd finished and her eyes bulged.

"Not yet. I'm taking my time and savoring every syllable. I'm such a huge fan," she said. "Is that weird that I said that? I know I see you all the time."

"Not at all," I replied with a soft grin.

I made myself comfortable in the window seat and am currently watching people scatter around on the street below while I wait for Luna to arrive. I love San Francisco. I love everything about it from the people to the hills. I especially love Luna's view of the ocean from this window. Every once in a while I stand and walk past the open door to see Brenna reading. Her reactions are food for my soul. One second she smiles, then she frowns. The next minute her hand is over her mouth, then she's fanning herself. I can't help but feel proud.

I think back to sitting in the Florida airport six months ago. It was about 7:00 a.m. by the time I made it through security and to my gate. There was a small part of me that was worried Fisher would follow me and an even bigger part of me that was sad he didn't. After a few minutes of sulking, I started thinking about him knocking me over on the beach. It made me laugh. It was a great story. I wanted to remember every second of our time together, so I opened my laptop and started typing what I remembered. My fingers flew across the keys effortlessly. There was so much I wanted to say. Then it hit me. This story needed an ending and I was going to create it. That's when the words really began to flow.

"Hey. Am I late or are you early?" Luna asks as she saunters into her office and pulls the scarf from around her neck.

"What do you think?" I reply as I take another sip of my coffee.

She drops her messenger bag by the side of her desk and walks over to me. She seizes the cup from my hands and takes a long drink. I smile up at her and run my fingers through my now long black hair, pulling at a small tangle.

"Oh, that's better." She sighs as she hands the cup back to me.

"Long night?"

She rolls her eyes. "Um, yeah! I couldn't sleep. I'm too excited. You look rested. How is that even possible? Why am I more nervous than you are?"

I take another sip. "Maybe because you'll make more money off of it than I will?"

"Ha! You're a riot." Luna plops down in her chair and shuffles some papers on her desk. I rotate the cup in my hands and watch her gaze at the clock on the wall. A slow smile spreads across my lips when she lifts the phone to her ear to check if there's a dial tone. She huffs as she carefully places it down and jiggles it to make sure it's in place.

"You're getting your hopes up for nothing," I tell her. "You and I both know that movie deals rarely work out. It's probably some small wannabe producer who's going to need a GoFundMe account just to buy a camera."

"Stop!" she says, spinning in her chair and holding out her finger to scold me. "Law of Attraction, remember? In the four months since *Book Boyfriend* released, you've had over thirty-six thousand reviews. You've been on the best seller list for months and we're starting to get interview requests. This is going to blow up just like I told you it would after I read the first chapter."

Her lips twist into a smug grin as she spins in circles in her chair. I shrug my shoulders like I don't care and gaze back out the window. I know it'll drive her nuts. I'm right.

"Are you fucking kidding me? Did you just shrug your shoulders?"

I laugh. "I'm just joking. You know I'm freaking out on the inside. This book has done more for my career than I ever imagined. Who knew so many people fantasized about a Penn Fitzgerald of their own?"

Luna twirls around in her chair slowly this time. "Ahh, Penn . . . I want a Penn. He's seriously the perfect man and obviously, by your phenomenal sales, everyone thinks so too. Who doesn't dream of meeting a sexy stranger on the beach, never exchanging names, and then having him read your book and track you down, wooing the shit out of you?"

I shrug again.

"Oh and having him be a billionaire playboy didn't hurt either."

There's a knock on the door. Brenna is leaning on the frame. "Please tell me Penn is real! Please!"

I wrinkle my nose. She's almost sobbing. "Sorry. He doesn't exist."

Brenna moans in pain and returns to her desk in the hall.

Luna stares at me, her eyes narrowing.

"What?" I ask, placing my coffee mug on the bench next to me.

"You and I both know he sort of does."

I shake my head. "Nope! Don't go there. We agreed that we would never, ever discuss this."

"I wish you'd just tell me his name again. I know his first name was Fisher. But Fisher what?"

"I honestly don't remember."

"You're a horrible liar. And can I just say that you're the only woman in the history of women who got fondled by the perfect man and then didn't even bother to Google him."

"My imagination is always better than reality. Why do you think so many women cling to their books? It's because we want a man like Penn to exist and to want us. I'd rather have my fabulous fiction over a disappointing reality any day."

Luna scratches her head and sighs. "You're seriously impossible."

Her direct line rings and we both stop and strain to listen as Brenna answers.

Brenna screams from the hall. "It's them!"

"Be calm. Act professional. Don't seem too eager. Pretend we get movie offers all the time. Don't jump on anything. Don't act interested. Or excited. Or bored. Or—"

"Luna?" I begin. "Stop talking to yourself and answer the phone."

She clears her throat, placing the call on the dreaded speakerphone she hates. "Luna Lord."

"Good morning, Luna. This is Fabian. Is this a good time?"

"Oh hi, Fabian. Sure. What can I do for you?"

"So we had a conference call this morning. Are you sitting down? Summit is prepared to negotiate."

My mouth drops, and I slowly slide to the floor.

"Summit? Like 'Twilight' Summit?" Luna asks calmly.

"That's the one. Do you think Macy will take a meeting to work out the details?"

"Um . . ." Luna gazes at me on the floor. Her expression tells me I must look like I'm about to pass out. It's exactly how I feel.

"I think we could definitely arrange something."

"They're prepared to let her review the script and help with casting. At least, that's usually what authors have requested in the past."

Luna lifts her eyebrows and motions to me for some visible sign that I'm alive. I hold my hand over my mouth to keep from screaming.

"Sounds great. Send me some dates and a location and I'll make sure she's there."

"We look forward to working with you, Luna. Congratulations. This is a once in a lifetime opportunity."

"Thanks, Fabian. Talk to you soon."

Luna ends the call and her head quickly pivots to regard me. She screams as she rushes over to me and pulls me to my feet.

"Oh my God, Luna! Is this real?"

"You bet your tight ass it is!"

We both jump up and down and squeal like school girls as we embrace. Brenna rushes into the room with a nervous expression and sees that we're both crying. As her eyes scan ours, she starts to cry right along with us. We find ourselves in a three-way hug.

Brenna sniffs out, "Are we happy or sad?"

"Summit!" I shout.

"You mean we're *had*. Like the sum of happy and sad?"

Luna grabs her cheek and kisses it. "You know what, Brenna? I'm not even upset that you don't know what we're talking about right now. I'm too freaking happy!"

"Ooh, we're happy! Yay!"

I can't help but laugh as Brenna claps excitedly and Luna stumbles over to her desk. "Brenna, get your purse! We're going out to dinner!"

"It's only nine thirty," I remind her. She stares at me blankly. "In the morning."

"Oh, right. Then breakfast! But wait." She pauses, pressing her finger to her lips. "This doesn't leave this office. Understood?" She points back and forth between us and we both nod. We know serious Luna when we see her.

"We will not jeopardize any of this by speaking out of turn. This is hush hush until the ink is dry!"

Luna's right. The reality of the situation hits me like a ton of bricks. I can't believe I let myself hope for something, even for a few seconds. That's not me. Nothing has been decided for sure. This could all fall apart. I slide back into my window seat. Every time I get my hopes up, I get disappointed. I refuse to believe. Not yet. Not ever.

CHAPTER 6

"What else can I get for you?" Brenna asks as she fluffs the pillows on the couch in my new office.

"I honestly don't know what I need."

Brenna wrings her hands and walks to the wall opposite my desk, straightening the rows of my books on the tall, white cases. When they are perfectly aligned she repositions the tulips on my desk. I watch her curiously. She stops when she sees me staring and peers out into the hall like she dreads leaving me.

"I'm really excited to have you here, even if it is only for a few months. Do you need anything?"

I shake my head.

"I'm just outside. Press zero and I'll come running."

I smile. She's really sweet. "Thank you. I think it's going to take me a little while to get used to this setup. Is Luna here yet?"

Brenna gazes up at the clock on the wall. Luna insists

there be one in every room. She doesn't like people constantly looking at their phones. She wants to know you're checking the time rather than reading a text. She's heard the checking the clock excuse way too many times. Now no phones are allowed during meetings. She runs a tight operation.

"It's not even nine. She's usually in about five minutes after. Half the staff rushes in at nine oh three."

I smirk. I should know that by now. I'm just glad Brenna is early like I am. It's nice to have someone here with me on my first day.

"Do you want more coffee?" she asks, pointing to my orange "Calm Your Tits" mug.

"No, I'm good for now. I've already had three cups and I'm either going to pee all day or shake uncontrollably. You go ahead and do whatever you need to do. I'm fine."

Brenna smiles and slowly backs out of my office. It's almost as if she thinks I'll disappear if she takes her eyes off me. Luna probably told her to make sure I don't make a run for it.

After we signed the contract to proceed with the movie for *Book Boyfriend*, Luna insisted I get an office at the publishing house. Once they get the script written, she says it'll be easier to communicate with them if I'm here rather than at home. I think she wants to keep an eye on me and make sure I'm working on the sequel.

I hate sequels. I thought I'd wrapped up the story nicely, but I guess readers want more of Penn and Kasey. The constant requests on social media along with the fifty thousand books I sold the first month made a sequel almost a necessity. Luna said it would be stupid to walk away from the potential sales a second book could bring.

I plop down in my desk chair and swivel around in a circle, ending back at the flashing cursor on the blank page of my laptop. Leaning my head on my hand, I stare at the screen.

I can barely remember the details of Fisher's eyes anymore and it makes me sad. I really wanted to move on from him, but since the last book did so well, I'll be forced to think about him for a few more months. I hate that I made him so damn perfect and part of me wishes I wouldn't have written about him at all. He's gone from my dreamy one-night fling to the man I've thought about obsessively for months. It wasn't supposed to be like that. I honestly believed I'd walk away from him and never think of him again. Boy, was I wrong.

Still, I refuse to Google him. I know it's silly, but I'd rather fantasize about him as the ideal man than find out he's a douche. I think if I searched him, it would ruin my chances of writing another book. I couldn't write Penn as the sexy alpha male he is if I found out Fisher wasn't like him at all. He's my muse.

But, I'd be lying if I said I hadn't thought about looking him up. I'd kill to see a picture of him. Deep down inside I know one image would be like my personal crack and I'd end up searching for him day and night until I knew everything there was to know.

I refuse to do it. Instead, I think about that one amazing night on the beach and try to let the rest go. Forgetting him would be easier if I had a man in my life, but I still have no desire to date. It's just me and my books. I'm fine with the way things are. At least, that's what I tell myself on lonely nights. No one needs to know that thinking about him is the only way I orgasm anymore. It's so pathetic. I need to get a life.

I tug my hair back and twist the tie around it until it's out of my face. I don't care what I look like. I usually don't think about it much unless I'm going to be around people I don't know.

When Luna insisted I come here three times a week, I told her that after today, she should expect me here in my pajamas. I can hardly wait to prove to her that I was serious. I'm about ready to take off these dress pants and sit in my underwear.

"See? Isn't this nice?"

Briefly lifting my eyes from the screen, I scowl at Luna as she stands in the doorway.

"That's an attractive look for you. Should I grab the camera? We can use that as the next image for the back of your books."

"Fuck off. I'm trying to write."

She practically skips to my desk and I grab the laptop away from her prying eyes before she sees the blank page.

"Oh come on!"

"No. You'll have to wait just like you do when I'm at home." I unbutton the top button of my pants and untuck my blouse to cover it.

"You look really nice today." She tries not to laugh when she says it, but she can't control herself.

"I'm wearing sweats on Wednesday. Be prepared."

"I don't care what you wear as long as I get to squeeze you once a day. It'll almost be like the old days when you were the first person I saw in the morning."

"First of all, we haven't roomed together since freshman year in college and that lasted a whole semester because I couldn't stand the constant influx of various men. I was rarely the first person you saw and we both know it."

"Minor details. Did you start an outline?"

I swallow hard and gaze at the door, searching for something to distract Luna from her question. "Did I mention that Brenna is a real sweetheart? You should give her a raise."

Luna furrows her brows and sits on the corner of my desk, crossing her arms. "Let me see what you've written."

"No. I'm not ready for you to read it yet."

She shakes her head. "You lie for shit. You haven't written anything, have you?"

I huff like I'm offended. "I'll have you know that I was about to type before you came barging in here."

She smirks. "You've got this. You know that, don't you?"

I smile weakly. "Of course."

She gazes up at the clock on the wall. "I have a conference call. I'll see you for lunch?"

"Yes. You're taking me out and you're buying."

As she leaves the office, I place my laptop back on my desk and grab ahold of the mouse, tapping it nervously. Where do I begin?

It's almost noon when Brenna knocks on my door. "Delivery!"

I quickly click on the close tab so she doesn't see or hear the video of the skating dog I was watching.

"Sorry to interrupt, but this came for you!"

The smell hits me almost immediately. My stomach growls as I open the bag she places on my desk: two steak tacos, a chicken taco, chips, and a big tub of guacamole.

I roll my eyes. "Ha! Tell Luna she's hilarious."

"Tell me I'm what?" she asks as she rounds the corner. "You ordered food? I thought we were going out?"

"I didn't order food, you did. Was this supposed to be funny? Are you trying to inspire me?" I ask.

"What did you get?"

"I got the meal Penn sends Kasey on her first day in the office. It's cute but a little creepy."

"Really?" Luna asks excitedly. "Is there a card?"

"You know perfectly well that Penn doesn't send a card. Kasey ends up calling the taco place and they tell her that a gentleman came in, paid cash, and asked that the food be delivered to her workplace."

"But did you get one this time?" she asks.

"You're not funny. Just admit you sent it. We can laugh about it and I might even share my chips."

"Greer . . . I swear I didn't do it. Maybe it was the production team?"

She's serious. I can tell. I shrug my shoulders. "Yeah, maybe." I empty the bag and as expected there's no card.

After I left Fisher in Florida, I started writing nonstop. I created this fantasy book where Penn ends up seeing a picture of Kasey on the news, realizes she's an author and reads her book. Then he starts making everything in the story come true. The first thing that happens is Kasey gets tacos. It would be funny if someone left a card saying it was a joke.

"The delivery guy asked specifically for Macy Greer," Brenna says after the brief silence.

"Brenna, can you call the taco place and see who ordered the food?" Luna asks.

"I'm on it."

Luna grabs a taco and sits down in the chair across from my desk. "It's kind of cute, don't you think?"

"Unless they're laced with poison from a crazy fan who

hates me. Maybe Selena Popper sent them. You know she tweeted that the world would be a better place with less of my whiny characters."

Luna stops mid bite and refolds the taco into the wrapper, placing it on my desk. "She's just jealous. She's never happy for anyone. I swear, her readers are made up of nothing but haters. I've never seen such a nasty group. But she'd never stoop so low as to kill you. Jeez, overreact much?"

"Why'd you stop eating then?" I ask through a smirk.

"I remembered I'm on Keto. No carbs."

"Uh-huh." I unwrap a taco and lift it to my lips. "So you wouldn't mind if your star writer ate a deadly taco and died before the sequel was written?"

"Stop! Don't eat that!"

I laugh. "Now who's paranoid?"

Luna stands and picks up the food and drops it in the trash. "I promised you we'd go out to lunch. Let's go."

I re-button my pants and slip my shoes back on my feet.

Brenna is just ending her call as we exit my office. Her eyes look like they might pop out of her head. "They said some guy in a three-piece suit came in and ordered the food. The girl said he was really cute. She also said he paid cash. It's just like the book!"

Luna and I stare at each other. Luna shrugs her shoulders. "Whatever. It's probably a fan who begged her husband to do it. You'll probably get a message from one of your readers asking if you liked it. You're more popular than ever. Weird shit is bound to happen."

I laugh although it's uneasy. She's probably right. Tacos are one thing. No one would dare do what Penn does next.

CHAPTER 7

I almost left the house in my sweats, but it felt too casual. I settled on yoga pants and a T-shirt. Writing only happens when I'm comfortable. I'm too easily distracted by a tight waistband. My characters are miserable and argue whenever I'm uncomfortable.

It's a Thursday and I'm technically not supposed to go in today, but I have this strange desire to be there. It's an odd experience for me, actually having somewhere to go every day.

Usually, I roll out of bed whenever I feel like it, think about showering but never do it, and wander around my apartment finding mundane things to focus on rather than writing. Forcing myself to get up and get going is somewhat refreshing. I only spent two hours yesterday looking at music videos rather than the entire day I spent Monday. I'd call that progress.

It's also kind of nice having other people around and the view is way more inspiring than my own. It doesn't hurt that Brenna is willing to move heaven and earth if I need a tissue, much less a refill of coffee. It makes me feel special. It's a new feeling for me and I'm afraid I could get used to it.

It's a forty-minute drive to the publishing house, but I just pop in an audiobook and time flies. I didn't force myself to get up early today to be there before nine. It's 10:00 a.m. when I leave the house and the lighter traffic makes me wonder why I rush other days to be there so early. It's not like anyone cares when I come in.

I'm about fifteen minutes away and at a juicy part in my audiobook when my phone rings. The number seems familiar, but it doesn't show up on my caller ID. I decide to answer it anyway via Bluetooth.

"Hello?"

"Macy? I mean Greer?"

"Who is this?"

"I'm so sorry to bother you, it's Brenna. I know you're not supposed to be here today, but, um . . . Is there any way you could get here? Like, really, super fast?"

"I'm actually almost there. I decided to come in today. Why? What's up?"

"Um . . . I don't know how to explain this."

There's some brief shuffling on the phone and mumbling in the background.

Luna's voice catches me off guard. "Get in here now! You're never going to fucking believe this!"

"What's going on?" I shout. Pressing my foot into the floorboard, the car quickly picks up speed. I'm starting to panic. "Did the movie deal fall through? Did they change their minds? I knew it was too good to be true."

"No! That's not it. When can you get here?"

"I'm probably like five minutes away now that I'm speeding. I was coming in anyway. Please tell me what's going on. I'm freaking out!"

Luna laughs. "It's not bad. It's unreal. Hurry the fuck up. Seriously. I'm dying."

"You're dying? What do you mean? Are you sick?"

"Not *that* kind of dying! Excited dying. Okay, I gotta go. They need me. Just hurry!"

She hangs up before I can say another word. She said "*They* need me" as in more than one. I fly into the parking lot and my tires screech as I slam on the brakes. Who are *they*? If it's not the movie people then who is it? The editing team? Photographers? Did they send models for me to look at? Ooh! I like that idea!

Running through the lobby, I decide to take the stairs when the elevator has a line. By the time I make it to the fourth floor, I'm significantly winded. Who knew wearing tennis shoes and yoga pants today meant I'd be getting a workout.

Brenna sees me coming and jumps up from her desk and cracks open the closed door of my office.

"I'm here! Someone tell me what the hell is going on!"

Luna squeezes out the door of my office like she's hiding something. The grin on her face reminds me of the day she screwed the quarterback in college. She was proud and bursting to give me all the details. From the look on her face today, I'd say she fucked the entire football team.

"I'm so glad you're here. You're never going to believe this!"

"What?" I drop my purse and my tote bag on Brenna's desk as I rush to my door. "Is it good or bad?" I ask before I open it.

"It's fucking amazing!" Luna begins. I hesitate. I'm not

good with surprises. Luna must recognize my fear because she says, "What's the second thing Penn does for Kasey in your book?"

My eyes narrow as I rack my brain to think. When it hits me, my eyes bulge. "No!" I shout.

Luna claps and I open my office door. Positioned in the corner is a string quartet in tuxedos: three violins and a cello. When I wrote this scene, I tried to think of something really romantic that any girl would love. So, in my story, Kasey writes about her fictitious boyfriend sending a string quartet to serenade her with her favorite classical music while she works.

"They just showed up!" Brenna shouts. Half the office has now gathered outside my door as I walk inside.

"This is Macy," Luna says, motioning to me.

The cello player nods to the others and they start to play. I slowly amble to my desk, completely aware that my mouth is hanging on the floor.

At first, I don't recognize the song. I'm not much of a classical girl. I just wrote Kasey as one because she's a little more sophisticated than I am. But as they play, I start to recognize the melody. It's not Bach, or Mozart, it's . . . Fall Out Boy? Are they playing "I Don't Care" on strings?

Tears sting my eyes. It's beautiful and crazy all at the same time. I slide into my desk chair, unable to take my eyes off them.

Their fingers move with grace and skill. If you didn't know any better you'd think they were playing a concerto rather than a rock song. As they play, more and more people from the office crowd into my room. We clap and roar at the end of the song. They move right into, "Sugar, I'm Going Down" and then "Irresistible."

Just as they're about to start another, I ask them to stop. I walk around my desk and over to them then I eye Luna. She reads my mind. Waving everyone out of the room, she closes the door behind the last person.

"I don't mean to be rude by interrupting, and you play magnificently, but I need to know. Who sent you?" I ask.

"We're not at liberty to say, miss. It's part of our contract."

"Your contract?"

"Yes, we were asked to play a variety of Fall Out Boy songs on strings for one hour, but we weren't allowed to begin until you arrived, no matter how long that took."

"But . . . why?" I ask. "Who would do this?"

The cello player seems to be in charge since he's the only one who speaks. He shrugs his shoulders to my question then says, "Shall we continue?"

My head rolls to regard Luna as my hands fly open in question to her. She can see I don't know what to do, so she pipes up.

"Are you allowed to tell us anything?"

He smiles. "I was told that the woman we were playing for was quite lovely and that this was her favorite band. That's all."

"Did you meet the person who contracted you?"

"No. We spoke on the phone."

"Man or woman?" Luna asks.

"Man."

"And how did he pay?" I ask, as if I don't already know the answer.

"He paid in cash. There was an envelope waiting with the signed agreement last night."

"Could you give me a minute?" I ask, pulling Luna by the elbow as we leave my office. She's smirking the whole way.

As soon as we're in her office, I close the door behind me. "This is awful!" I moan, placing my fingers over my eyes and leaning my back against the door.

"No, it's not! It's fantastic! Someone is following your book to the letter! Well, except for the choice of music."

"That's just it! How did they know my favorite music?" My mind wanders back to the day on the beach with Fisher and my ratted T-shirt. I swallow hard.

"Duh?" Luna says as she rolls her eyes. "You post about them all the time. You recorded half their songs on your Instagram feed when you went to their concert, remember? Anyone who knows you, knows you love them."

I teeter my head. She's got a point. A quick search on my Facebook, Twitter, and Instagram accounts and you'd see I talk about them more than my own books.

"And you swear to the creator of dildos and dicks that this is not you?"

She lifts her right hand and places the other on her heart. "I swear. If I'm lying I'll never have sex again."

She's serious. She'd never say that unless it was the absolute truth. "Do you really think it's just a fan? I mean, that shit costs money!"

"I do. Think about it. Whoever sent them had no clue you weren't working today. No one knew you were coming but you. If it was someone we knew, someone we worked with, like, say, the movie team, they'd know you only worked Monday, Wednesday, and Friday. Whoever sent it didn't make sure you'd be here first. That's kind of dumb when you think about it."

I nod.

"Stop worrying about it and just enjoy."

"In the book, Kasey thinks it's a fan and it's not. It's Penn. What if this is . . . him?"

Luna stands up straighter. "The Fish guy?"

I nod once more.

Luna laughs. "No way. What would be the chances? You said you gave him your real name not your author name, right?"

"Yes."

"And he had no clue what you did for a living?"

"No."

She waves me off. "It's a fan."

I furrow my brows and hug myself.

"What comes next?" Luna grabs my book off her shelf and I start biting at my nails as I try to remember. "The dress!"

She starts to clap. "Doesn't he show his face then too? Girl . . . this stuff is gold!"

Walking over to her window, I slide down into the seat. Fear hits me hard. "What if it's a stalker? Did you think of that?"

Luna's face turns white. She immediately picks up her phone. "Brenna, get Fabian on the line."

The phone rings and she faces me as she speaks. "Fabian, I'm going to need the best private security you can find and I need it today."

CHAPTER 8

I t's odd always having someone with me, but I also feel so much better when Marcus is around.

Within an hour of Luna's call to Fabian, the production team had sent the owner of the security firm they use to her office for a consult. Part of me was worried I was overreacting, but when Luna explained what had happened to him and he seemed concerned, I felt validated.

I was immediately paired with Marcus. He's a tall, house of a man. He looks like he eats fear for breakfast, but when he smiles it's a lot less intimidating. I don't think he smiles much, though. He came over to my place and helped set up a security system and even gave me a panic button for my key chain that sends both the police and him running. I might sleep with it on my nightstand. I might be crazy, too.

It's been a week since my personal concert and nothing else has happened. Marcus meets me every time I have to leave the house. It's weird giving him my schedule and having to stick to it.

He went grocery shopping with me the other day and I only bought one bag of Sour Patch Kids because I felt like he might judge me for buying three. I'm a writer, though, and we writers need our snacks. Snacks and words go hand in hand. Too bad I ate them while I watched TV rather than writing. Now I'm out of luck.

Last night, I had a craving for Taco Bell and I wanted to run out to get it, but I ended up eating stale cereal instead because I freaked myself out of leaving the apartment.

I pictured myself thinking I'd be safe this one time without Marcus and then encountering a crazy stalker with a large machete. Isn't that how people die in movies? They take a risk and then they get kidnapped and chopped into pieces. Or for authors, tied to a bed and forced to write like in "Misery." As a viewer, you're sitting there screaming at your TV, telling them not to do it, but they go anyway.

I didn't want to be a stupid victim, so I stayed home. Unfortunately my irrational thinking continued the rest of the night and I barely slept. Once my damn brain gets going, I can't turn it off.

People may think it's fun being creative. They may think having an overactive imagination is a blessing. And while I'll admit, it's a great trait when you're writing at your laptop, it's not so great when you're sitting alone in your apartment and you overthink every little noise you hear.

I'd managed to convince myself that I heard a tap on my fourth story window. Then I pictured a man dressed in black scaling down from the roof to get a glimpse of me as I lay in bed. I invented his backstory and pictured the *20/20* episode where they reveal how they caught him. I think I got two hours, tops.

So, as I stagger into my office this morning with Marcus, I know I look as bad as I feel. At this rate, my sequel is going to turn into a thriller. I need to think romance not murder.

Brenna hands me a cup of coffee as soon as I sit down. I mouth the words "Thank you" to her because, truth be told, I'm too tired to speak.

After staring out my window for way too long, I finally start to feel semi human enough to write. I manage a thousand words before Brenna knocks on my door.

"Greer, you got something."

She walks through the door carrying a rather large box and Marcus follows her. He's stationed outside in case I need him during the day and he's never come inside before. The fact he's walking with her has my arm hairs standing at attention.

"Should I get Luna?" Brenna asks.

"I don't know." I gaze at Marcus and he motions for Brenna to give him the box.

"If it's okay with you, Ms. Greer, I'd like to open this myself."

I nod in approval and Brenna bolts out the door. Luna rushes in a few seconds later.

We stand a few feet from Marcus and cringe like the box might explode when he uses his pocket knife to slice open the tape.

He puts on a pair of latex gloves as he unfolds a letter, reads it, and then proceeds to remove a black sequin gown from the box. He grins. "We're going to get him now."

"Can you read it out loud?" I ask.

He clears his throat. "Your presence is requested for dinner tonight at The Chateau on Market Street at eight p.m. I will have a table reserved in your name and will wait for you to arrive. Consider the dress a gift, not a requirement."

Luna gasps. "Well, shit. It's the exact words from the book except for the restaurant. The Chateau is here in San Francisco. It's about three blocks away. It's a really nice place. At least you'll have a good meal," she says with a shrug.

"She's not going," Marcus announces. "We'll be there waiting for him instead and we'll grab him. There's no need for you to be present."

"Like hell I'm not going!" I reply, folding my arms. "In the book, Penn makes sure Kasey is there before he shows himself. If he doesn't see me, he might not go through with it."

"That's a chance we'll have to take."

"He probably read the story. I want to go. I want answers. I can't take this anymore. This whole thing is making me paranoid. I'm going and there's nothing you can say to stop me."

"Ms. Greer, I highly suggest you—"

"She's right," Luna interrupts. "And in the book Kasey goes alone. This guy won't be expecting security, but he won't approach unless he sees her sitting at the table. Once he identifies himself as the stalker, then you can pounce. Otherwise, what's to stop him from just walking away when he sees she's not there? You'll have no proof and no grounds. Plus, it's a busy restaurant."

"Maybe. But I don't want him getting that close."

"I can handle it!" I tell him. "And I'll give you some kind of sign when I know it's him. Otherwise, it could just be a fan and you'll give yourself away."

I gaze over at Luna as I speak and she nods in agreement. We both turn to face Marcus, who seems a little dazed.

He runs his fingers through his hair as he glances back and forth at us. "Have you two done this before? You seem to have this thought out."

I smile. "You have no idea how gratifying that is to hear."

Luna smirks and leans against the wall smugly.

"Am I missing something?" he asks.

Sitting in my desk chair, I roll forward until I can place my elbows on the desk. "We spent a lot of time on the particulars of this scene in the book so it seemed realistic. We ran a lot of scenarios."

"I see," he says with a small grin. "Let me think about it. Don't do anything until you hear back from me."

Once he's gone and my door is closed, Luna and I face each other, completely dumbfounded.

"Well, this has taken an interesting turn." Luna walks over to the dress and lifts it out of the box. "Want to try it on?"

"Hell no. I'm not wearing that thing. He probably jacked off all over it."

"Eww. That's gross. And Penn didn't. It looks clean . . . and pricey. Kasey wore it. She thought it was beautiful."

"We both know I'm not Kasey. Kasey was trusting until she realized he was the reason she became a best seller." Doubt invades my brain. "You don't think my stalker bought ten thousand copies too, do you?"

"No!" Luna says, shaking her head. "This is real life, darling. Men like Penn don't exist, remember?"

I know she's right. Penn doesn't exist. Real men are nothing like the ones in my head. Real men lie and cheat and break your heart. Book boyfriends will always be better than reality.

CHAPTER 9

“ A re you clear on what you're supposed to do?” Marcus asks, as he places a pin containing a small camera on my sweater. He's recording the whole thing in case we need it for a court case.

"Yes. When I know it's him, I stand up."

He places his hands on his thighs, leaning toward me. "You know it's not too late to change your mind."

Even though I'm nervous, I'm also pretty excited. It feels like I'm playing a part in a crime drama. I've already plotted a book off this whole thing about an undercover detective who falls for the guy she's supposed to be investigating. I'm trying to pretend I'm not scared because I know Marcus wouldn't let me go through with it if he knew I wasn't half as confident as I appear to be.

I suppose with popularity comes increased risk. When I first became a best seller, I paid a company to wipe my past personal stuff from the web mostly so I could keep my address safe. Looking back, especially since we're divorced, I'm glad I didn't take Oliver's name. Greer Bruckner never sat well with me anyway. Now, it's nearly impossible to know that Greer Hanson ever existed. I guess security and stalkers are the things I never considered when I prayed for fame.

"I'm not going to change my mind. Besides, you have like twenty other guys stationed all around this place. I'm not the slightest bit worried."

"Please reconsider the vest."

I inhale a deep breath through my nostrils to try to stay calm. The suggestion of my wearing a bulletproof vest almost made me cry when he mentioned it the first time. If it's going to happen, it'll happen. I'll die someday, vest or not. "Nope. I'm good."

Marcus arranged for a guard at the door and one sitting at the table near me. He's going to be standing at the bar, within feet of me. Luna wanted to be here, but he said no and I agreed. I don't need her taking any risks.

I'm directed to the table my stalker/gift giver reserved. I rub my hands on my jeans. My palms are sweaty. I semi-sing Eminem's song "Lose Yourself" as soon as the thought crosses my mind. Another one of my issues. I tend to think of song lyrics when I'm nervous.

This dude might expect me to be in the dress he bought me, but I'm not Kasey and my not wearing the dress like she did should drive that point home even further. Part of me hopes a smiling fan shows up and just asks for my autograph. Then Marcus can give her a restraining order and we can call it a day.

I watch the condensation drip down my water glass and realize the sweat on my back is following the same pattern. I keep glancing back and forth between the door and Marcus.

He nods to me as he holds a glass of soda and perches half a butt cheek on the bar stool.

A tap on my shoulder startles me and I almost bolt from my seat. "Excuse me, but aren't you Macy Greer?" a young woman asks as she steps in front of me.

Is this her? Is this it? Should I stand?

"Are you the person I'm meeting?" I ask hesitantly.

"I wish. I'm so sorry for bothering you, but my mom and I saw you when you came in and it took me a few minutes to get the courage to ask for your autograph."

I smile. "Um, sure. What do you want me to sign?"

She hands me a napkin and I gaze over at Marcus and shake my head lightly. I try to smile as I scribble my name.

"I love Kasey. She's like, my favorite character of all time. I love how feisty and sexy she is. I wish I could be more like her."

"Just be you. The world needs you to be exactly who you are and no one else."

She grins. "Thank you so much. Have a great dinner."

I watch her walk back to her table and I wave to the older woman she's sitting with. She smiles back.

Where the hell is he? I know I'm early, but jeez. Why is he late? Let's get this show on the road. People really need to be more punctual. It's rude to keep me waiting.

I try to busy myself by taking in the décor. You never know when I might need to describe a restaurant in a book. The walls are a deep shade of red. I suppose it's to match the exposed brick on the wall by the fireplace in the corner. It's a nice place. And I might have even thought it was a romantic location if I were on a date rather than waiting to meet a crazy person.

Why would anyone think I'd be interested in recreating a story in my book? I've written twelve other novels and no one copied those. I wish they would have. It would have been nice to inherit a million dollars from someone for real.

The door opens and I see the arm of what appears to be a suit. My lip begins to tremble as I try to remind myself that it could be a patron and not my mystery man.

My leg muscles tighten as I prepare to run. I should have worn the vest.

It's like time is moving in slow motion as he rounds the corner from the door. The first thing I see is the navy blue tie against a white shirt, covered in a dark gray suit. As I swallow hard, my eyes slowly travel up his chest to his broad shoulders. Is he walking toward me or is it my imagination?

I summon the courage to make eye contact and feel as if someone punched me hard in the gut. He's smiling. His teeth are white and perfect and his hair is even better than in my memories. I gasp and jump to my feet as excitement rushes from my toes to my chest in a wave of heat, utter joy, and complete relief.

"Fisher!" His smile grows even wider in my recognition. Is he here to save me from my stalker?

As my mouth opens with the intention of asking him why he's here, a blur of dark suits blazes forward out of the corners of my eyes. Like the petals of a flower encasing a bee as it's about to suck nectar, I watch as Fisher is surrounded and knocked to the ground, his legs flying out from under him in the process.

"No!" I shout. "It's not him!"

Marcus pulls Fisher's arms to his back and his beautiful perfect face is smashed against the hardwood floor.

I rush from the table over to him and immediately push a guard away so I can kneel next to him. His nose is bleeding.

"Oh my God!" I lean down to get closer to him.

"You could have at least let me buy you dinner before you crushed me," he says.

My grimace slowly fades away. He's still smiling even with a bleeding nose and his face pressed into the ground.

"Hi," I say. "Come here often?"

Marcus pulls him by the arms to a standing position.

"I've never been, but I have to say, the staff isn't very friendly," he replies as he's yanked upward.

"You stood up!" Marcus says as he cuffs Fisher's hands behind his back.

"I know, but it's not him. I just haven't seen him in a really long time and I, well, I got excited."

Fisher smirks and I regret my choice of words.

Marcus huffs and scowls at me. "How do you know it's not him?"

How *do* I know? Would he have done all this? Maybe this isn't a coincidence after all. Anger boils under my skin as I turn my head to him. "Was it you?"

"Can I ask what we're referring to?"

"The tacos, the Fall Out Boy musical experience, this damn dinner. The dress?"

His lips curl into a crooked smile. "You know, you're even beautiful when you're angry."

"Answer the question!"

Marcus pulls on his arms, causing Fisher to wince.

"Surprise?" He poses it like a question. "You didn't like it?"

I encase my head in my hands as my mouth drops to the

floor. I turn and pace back and forth a couple of times before I stop and place my hands on my hips. "You scared the shit out of me. Are you crazy? Are you seriously mental?"

"You started our story. I wanted to make it real."

I close my eyes.

"What do you want me to do?" Marcus asks.

I sigh as I watch the blood drip down Fisher's lips and onto his white shirt. I grab a napkin from the table and place it on his nose. "Let him go."

"You can't be serious!" Marcus mumbles in disbelief. "We caught him. Don't you want to press charges so this whole nightmare can be over?"

I dab Fisher's nose as I gaze into brown pools of chocolate with peanut butter streaks of gold. This is exactly what I was afraid of. I was so worried he was going to turn out to be a psychopath. But as I look into those eyes, my heart softens. He doesn't look crazy to me. He looks sincere and almost cocky. He doesn't seem the least bit worried that I'm going to press charges. Why is that?

"I'm sorry I scared you. It was never my intention. I figured you'd know it was me from when I had them play Fall Out Boy. You know, the T-shirt you dug out of the trash when you won an all-inclusive stay in Florida?"

Marcus rolls his eyes and frowns as he stares at me. I know nothing would please him more than to haul Fisher off to jail.

"Everyone knows I like Fall Out Boy! Why couldn't you just call me like a normal human being?"

"Well, if someone had given me their real number, then maybe I would have."

My lips purse. He got me on that one.

Marcus pulls tighter on his arms as Fisher tries to step toward me. Fisher's face strains and I panic at the thought that he's hurt.

"Can I explain?" he asks.

I'm probably a fool for wanting to hear him out. "Take the cuffs off. I want to talk to him in private."

"Ms. Greer, I highly suggest you reconsider."

A flashing light catches my eye toward the window and I see one of Marcus's men speaking with an officer. I turn my head and notice multiple phones out recording the event.

"Oh my God." I face Fisher once more and whisper, "Why does every encounter I have with you have to be a public spectacle?"

"Believe me when I say this is not what I had in mind."

An officer walks into the restaurant. "Let's get him down to the station."

"Marcus. No." I insist.

He shakes his head before it falls in frustration. "It seems my client doesn't want to press charges at this time."

He unlocks the cuffs and Fisher massages his wrists.

The officer frowns. "I need a full report right now."

Marcus whispers to Fisher, "I'm watching you." He turns and leads the officer out of the building, talking the whole way.

I turn to the crowd. "Show's over, folks."

Fisher adds, "Soon to be in theaters."

As people slowly move back to their tables, I close my eyes to get a grip. This is not how I pictured this night.

"Can we talk?" he whispers, leaning in.

I hand him the napkin for his nose. "Not here."

As I walk out of the restaurant and sit on a bench outside,

I gaze up and notice Marcus watching me carefully. It makes me feel better to know he still has my back even though he's pissed.

"May I join you?" Fisher asks, standing next to me, gazing down.

I nod. He rubs his nose lightly with the napkin and balls it up in his hands as he sits down.

"I had no idea you'd be scared."

"Really? Why wouldn't I be?" I ask as I face him. "Some stranger is reenacting my book and sending me gifts. I know nothing about you. Why would I consider it was you even for a second? I haven't thought about you in forever. And even if I had, why would I still not be scared out of my mind?"

His eyes furrow. "I'll deal with the part about you not thinking of me in a second. But first, are you trying to tell me you never once Googled me? Never looked up my Facebook profile or tried to find me on Instagram?"

"Not once."

His head rolls back in surprise. "Wow. You really aren't like other girls, are you?" He sighs when I cross my arms and turn away from him.

"A close friend of mine was bragging about this incredible book she read called *Book Boyfriend*. She wouldn't stop talking about it. One day when I was waiting for a flight to New York, I found myself with a little extra time. I wandered into a store and saw the book on a shelf. Greer isn't a name you hear every day. Out of curiosity, I picked it up and flipped it over. Imagine my surprise when I saw your photo."

I shrug half-heartedly. "It's not like I lied about anything. We never discussed what I did for a living."

"I know that. I figured you gave me a fake name along

with a fake number. I searched for you, you know. I regretted my decision to not go to the airport that morning after the phone number turned out to be for a pizza place."

My heart skips a beat. I remember feeling sad he didn't come that morning. It makes me feel better to know he was even considering it.

"I read it."

My head rotates abruptly to look at him as my eyes bulge. He read it? The book? Oh shit.

"I stood in that store and read the first chapter. I'm not gonna lie. I was flattered."

I stand and straighten my sweater as I gaze down the road. "Well, don't be. You gave me an idea, but the story isn't about you in the least."

He tries not to smile as his lips press together and he nods. I see his tongue push into his cheek. He doesn't believe me. I'm the worst liar in the world.

"So it's a coincidence that Penn Fitzgerald has the same initials as I do?"

"Huh. I never even considered it." I attempt conviction in my voice, but I'm sure I fail miserably.

He leans back on the bench and places his left arm on the edge. He tugs at his tie with his free hand to loosen it. "Regardless, it made me happy. Happy because I finally had a name to go with a face."

"I didn't lie to you. My real name is Greer Hanson. I just don't use it when I write."

"I realize that. And I also know you've written twelve other books. Very impressive. I'm working my way through them in chronological order."

"What? Why?" I ask.

"Because I want to know more about you. Reading your words makes me feel more in tune with you. I'm guessing there's a part of you in every story. I'm starting to feel more familiar."

I push up the sleeves of my sweater to avoid meeting his gaze and realize I'm still wearing the pin. I pull it off and stuff it into my pocket. I can't believe he's reading my books. In all the time we were married, Ollie never finished a single one. He claimed to have tried but said they weren't his thing. "You're a romance reader, huh? Who knew?"

He looks at me through the tops of his eyes and squints a little. I feel a flutter in my stomach. "I am now."

I try to toughen up. I don't want him to think his good looks and charm are affecting me. "To be honest, all you've done is confirmed that you really are a stalker. Maybe I should get a restraining order after all."

"Nah. I'm mostly harmless."

"Mostly . . . That's not even funny."

He stands and moves a step closer. "I think if you search your memories, Macy Greer, you'll remember you weren't scared of me at all on the beach."

After our eyes meet briefly I immediately turn my head and focus on the officers by the entrance to the restaurant. I wasn't scared of him on the beach and I'm not scared of him now. What I'm really afraid of is his proximity and my will-power.

He reaches out and moves a strand of my hair away from my mouth. "Your hair is longer. It's sexy. I like it. I'd like to see what it looks like splayed across my chest in the morning."

I gulp. "What did you say?" I yell to Marcus. "Oh sure, I'll be right there."

I scurry away from Fisher and his panty melting words and pretend Marcus called me. Marcus does a double take when I say his name and walks toward me.

"What's up? Did you change your mind?" he asks, cracking his knuckles and eyeing Fisher over my shoulder.

I shake my head. "No, no. I just need you to do me a favor. Can you check him out? Tell me if I should be worried?"

"Absolutely."

As he pulls out a pad of paper to write down his name, I take another look at Fisher. He's standing with his back to me, hands stuffed in his pockets.

I can't believe he's really here. What do I do now?

CHAPTER 10

"And then you left? Are you insane?"

I lean forward and place my head on top of my crossed arms to hide my face on my desk. "What was I supposed to do? Say, sure, let's go back to your place and I'll flip my hair all over your muscled abs?"

"Umm . . . Yes!"

I raise a finger out from the side of my head and flick Luna off.

She sighs loudly. "Well, the good news is that the videos people have posted on YouTube only show the back of your head. We were able to deny it was you."

"I signed an autograph."

"Don't worry about it. I think we're good."

"But Fisher's face is everywhere!"

"Okay, you have to tell me now. What's Fisher's last name?"

"Fisher is his last name."

"His name is Fisher Fisher? That's odd."

I lift my head off my arms and clench my teeth. "Are you for real? No. His last name is Fisher. His first name is Patrick. There's no use hiding it now."

"Move," Luna says as she pushes the arm of my chair, rolling me away from my desk. Her fingers fly over the keys. Within a second a picture of Fisher flashes on the screen. He's wearing a towel and his skin is drenched like he just stepped out of the shower. He also has that smoldering look on his face that made me stop breathing on the beach.

"Holy shit-tits! Is that him?" she asks.

I roll closer to the desk, pushing Luna to the side to get a better look.

"Patrick Fisher is a model turned actor, age thirty, from Cleveland, Ohio."

I click on the "images" tab and picture after picture of him appears on my screen. This is what I've been missing? I should have checked him out sooner. Holy hell. If I had seen these pictures a month ago I would have had a trilogy written by now.

"He doesn't look like Chris Hemsworth," Luna adds. "It's Henry Cavill."

I snap my fingers at her. I knew he reminded me of someone.

"He's hot as fuck. You weren't kidding there." Luna pushes my hand away and goes back to "all" to scroll more info on him.

"Girl, it doesn't look like he's ever been married. He's dated, but who hasn't?"

"Okay, that's enough. I don't want to see or hear anything else about him. I don't care." I stand and walk away from the desk.

"Oh, here's a picture of him naked!"

"What?" I rush back over to the screen, angling it toward me, and Luna laughs. It's him in a suit but not the birthday suit I was expecting.

"Uh-huh. You don't care. You wanted to see what kind of package the future father of your children was carrying."

"Stop. And I already saw his package, remember?"

"So did you describe it to the T? Does he manscape? Inquiring minds want to know."

"Knock it off!" I laugh, covering my face with my hands.

The phone buzzes. "Yes?" Luna asks.

"Marcus Montgomery is here."

"Send him in."

Marcus walks through the door with a file in his hand and immediately opens it on the desk in front of me.

"Patrick Fenton Fisher, age thirty, born and raised in Cleveland, Ohio. Graduated from Columbia School of the Arts in New York. Started modeling at age eighteen when he was discovered in a Starbucks as a barista. Modeled for Ford, did ads and runways all over the world for years. He's been in two movies, small roles, numerous commercials, and is currently working on location in Fresno filming twelve episodes of a new series due to be aired on *Fox* next season. He travels a lot. As far as a criminal history, he was given community service for public intoxication when he was twenty-one. Other than that, he's squeaky clean. Too clean if you ask me."

I fold my arms over my chest and lean forward to look at the file. "So no priors for stalking? No restraining orders?"

"Just because someone hasn't been arrested for it, doesn't mean they haven't done it. He probably hasn't been caught yet."

"His initials are PFF." Luna makes the sound rather than saying the letters. "I like him already."

"Thank you, Marcus. I really appreciate you doing this for me."

He nods. "So you know, after you left, the police asked him if he wanted to press charges against us. He said no, but I don't think he's done with this. I suggest you still file a restraining order. I don't think he should be allowed anywhere near you ever again."

Luna does a double take at him then stares at me. I suddenly feel uncomfortable. I don't know how I feel about never seeing him again. As if she's read my mind, Luna speaks.

"Marcus, you've done an amazing job these last couple of weeks and I think I can speak for both Macy and myself when we say we're grateful for everything. The thing is, now that Macy realizes that Fisher is harmless and that this whole thing has been a complete misunderstanding, I think it's safe to say that, for now, we won't be requiring your services any longer."

"What? But—"

Luna walks around the desk and grabs him by the elbow, leading him toward the door. "I will definitely tell Fabian what an outstanding job you've done and I promise we'll call you for any publicity events we have in the future."

Marcus turns to look at me over his shoulder and I lift my hand and wave at him as I smile awkwardly.

Luna closes the door behind him and leans on it. "Phew."

"Thank you. But do you really think Fisher *isn't* a threat?"

"I think he's romantic. Who wants safe? A little danger and intrigue is intoxicating."

I shake my head and sit down at my desk. Clapping my

hands together first, I place my hands back on my keyboard. "Okay, so now that this whole mess is finally over, can we just go back to my trying to write and you bugging me about doing it faster?"

"If that's what you want."

"It is. I want to forget any of it ever happened. I want to forget all about him." Right after I write another book about him.

I'm pretending to enjoy eating carrots for a snack when Brenna knocks at my door. I gaze up at the clock. It's already after three. This day has flown by.

"Come in."

"Hi, so, um, are you accepting appointments here?" she asks.

"Appointments? For what?" The cracking sound as I bite into another carrot is louder than I thought it would be. Even my chewing sounds louder now that someone else is in the room. Weird. I continue to type, not even looking at Brenna. I'm on a roll today.

"A lunch meeting, I guess?"

"With who? The producers usually go through Luna."

"No, not the producers. With the . . . book guy."

My head pops up and Brenna smiles nervously. "The book guy?"

"He's on line one. He asked if he could make a lunch appointment with you tomorrow. You know, just like in the story."

My face tightens. Is he for real? I drum my fingers on my

desk. "Put him through, please."

Brenna scurries away and I stare at my phone, waiting for it to ring. As soon as it does I lift the receiver and let loose. "You can't be fucking serious?"

"Well, hello there. I don't remember Kasey picking up the phone. I'm pretty sure she just said no."

"This isn't a book, Fisher, and I'm not Kasey."

He laughs lightly. "And thank God you're not. I had a dog growing up named Casey and that would be really weird for me."

I try my hardest not to smile. He's not cute. He's not. "What do you want?"

"You didn't really think I was going to let you walk away and never talk to you again, did you?"

"Look, I have no interest in dating you."

He laughs. "Good. I think dating is overrated. I think we should hang out, not date."

"I don't want to hang out with you either."

"Are you sure about that?"

"Yes."

"Hmm . . . that's weird. I was thinking about how excited you were to see me yesterday. I'm guessing if those hulks of yours hadn't pushed me to the floor, I probably would have gotten, at minimum, a hug. Maybe even a kiss."

"I don't want to kiss you either."

"Not even a tiny little peck on the cheek?"

"No. Not even that. I don't like you."

He laughs again. "What's the saying about someone who protests too much?"

"I'm speaking the truth. I'm sorry if that hurts your tender ego."

"Ouch," he says with a snicker. "I knew going into this you were going to be hard to crack. I've always liked that about you. The fact is, I really didn't get much of a chance to talk to you yesterday. All I'm asking for is one meal. If after that you still want me to leave you alone, then I will. Deal?"

"How about if you just leave me alone now?"

"I suppose I could do that, but what fun would that be? Don't you feel the least bit bad about the bruised ego I now have to go along with my bruised face?"

Squeezing my eyes shut, I remember his bloody nose. "Are you okay? I'm really sorry about all that."

"Are you?"

"Of course I am. I didn't want you to get hurt."

"What if it would hurt me if you wouldn't have dinner with me?"

I sigh. "Are you trying to play on my guilt to get me to cave?"

"Is it working? If it is, then yes. My nose really hurts."

I can't help but grin. I roll my chair around so I can look out the window. "How do I know you aren't crazy?"

"Aren't we all? Listen, if you had given me your real number months ago, I would have called you the next day to arrange to see you. I told you back then I wanted to see you again. Why are you surprised?"

"Because of the book stuff."

"Was it that bad? You didn't like it at all?"

I think for a minute. "I guess it did make me smile, up until the part where I was scared for my life."

He moans. "Please let me make it up to you."

I want to say no just for the sake of saying no, but if I'm honest with myself, seeing him again has been on my mind since before I even walked away from him yesterday. He's been on my mind for months. "What did you have in mind?"

"Do you trust me enough to give me your cell number?"

"Not really but . . ."

"But?"

I rattle off the numbers because I kind of want his number too.

"I'll text you tomorrow with the address. Just do me one favor?"

"What?"

"Let your GPS lead you. Don't overthink it. And dress casual."

My skin buzzes with nervous energy. "Are you always going to be secretive?"

"Always makes me think there are going to be a lot more dates. I like how you're thinking."

I try to change the subject. "It better be a public place."

He laughs. "It will be."

"I have to work. See you tomorrow, I guess."

"Nothing will make me happier. Goodbye, Greer."

Ending the call, my heart pounds wildly in my chest. What's wrong with me? Before I met him I would have never agreed to any of this. What is it about him that makes me so not *me*?

CHAPTER 11

L ast night, Fisher texted me an address along with a time. It's not quite 6:00 p.m. when my GPS leads me to a small airport just outside of town. Oh no.

I park my car in the lot and lean forward in my seat to watch a small aircraft take off in the distance. I should have known better. He couldn't possibly still be following the book. Could he?

There's a tap on my window and it startles me. I jump a little and Fisher grins outside my door. "Are you coming?" he asks.

I shake my head. He tries to open my car door. It's locked.

He bends down to look me in the eyes. "I promise you, it's going to be fine."

He's so sincere. Why didn't I Google the address? Why did I trust him? I've made up my mind as I open the door. "No. No way," I say adamantly as I step out.

"How about we start with hi instead of no."

He's wearing dark jeans and a blue shirt. He looks like he's about to get his picture taken. I glance down at the jeans it took me forever to pick out and wish I'd dressed up a little more. Even though he said casual, and he's dressed casually, he still looks way better than I do. "Okay. Hi. Now no!"

"Give me your hand and come with me."

"Please tell me you don't own your own plane like Penn? Because I can tell you right now, I'm not flying to Denver for dinner."

"Can you let me do this? I promise you, you'll have all the answers you need in a few minutes."

I glance over at the terminal. What do I do? Fisher takes my hand in his and walks backward, walking me with him. "It's going to be fun, I promise."

My phone rings and from the sound, I know it's Luna. There's no way I'm talking to her now even though I promised her I'd call her the minute I arrived. I silence the ringer as I notice the time. It's not quite six. "Are you actually early for once?" I ask, surprised.

"I've been here for a couple of hours."

"You have? Why?"

"I didn't want you to have to sit through all the paperwork and pre-flight stuff."

"So we *are* flying?"

"Yes."

I stop dead in my tracks and turn to walk back to my car.

He laughs and chases after me. "You don't even know what I have planned. Don't make me carry you over there."

"You wouldn't dare."

"Want to try me?"

He's serious. Would he really pick me up? "I'm not saying yes. So we're clear."

"Crystal." He holds out his hand and I place mine inside. We walk over to a gentleman standing with a clipboard. "She's here," he tells him.

The man smiles and holds his hand out to me. "I'm Phil."

"Macy," I say, shaking his hand.

"Phil is a friend of a friend. He's going to help me out today."

"With what?" I ask, still concerned.

"Shall we go?" Phil asks.

As he starts to walk, I pull on Fisher's arm. "Really. I'm scared. Are we really flying today?"

He knows I'm serious. "In your book, you write that Penn is not only a millionaire, but also has his own plane. He takes Kasey up and personally flies her to Denver for dinner."

"I'm fully aware of my own story."

He grins as he stuffs his hands into his pockets and glances toward Phil, then back to me. "I'm not exactly a millionaire and I don't own my own jet, but I arranged for my first flying lesson with Phil today and he said I could bring you along. Then I brought a picnic basket and I thought we could eat dinner over there and watch the planes take off for a while. It's the closest I could get."

Dead. I'm dead. I'm pretty certain his words were like an ice pick shattering any pre-conceived notions about what kind of man he was. It is the sweetest thing anyone has ever done in my life.

"Are you okay?" he asks. "You're white as a ghost. I promise you, Phil knows what he's doing. He flies for Southwest. I wouldn't let anything happen to you."

All these memories of Florida invade my mind. Fisher's

panicked face as he lay on top of me in the sand. Fisher insisting on carrying my bag to the hotel. His hot breath on my neck asking if I wanted a taco. My undoing the zipper of his shorts in the ocean. He's here. The guy I've thought about nonstop for months. The guy I based an entire book on is standing right in front of me trying to make me smile. How could I ever not follow him anywhere? "Promise?"

His returning smile makes my knees weak. "I promise."

We walk to a small plane on a paved strip. "Patrick already did the pre-flight check before you arrived and we walked through the checklists. He said you might be nervous, so I wanted to personally assure you we're good to go."

I nod as he hands me a headset and I climb into the back seat of a small plane. I immediately buckle my seatbelt.

"This is a Cessna C-172. It's a plane we use for training."

Fisher climbs in the front seat and puts on a pair of sunglasses along with a headset. He turns back to me and smiles. "Ready?"

I want to scream yes and throw my body at him, but I'm not sure Phil would appreciate that. Could he be any hotter than he is right at this moment? Mother of mercy, if I could I'd go back and rewrite this scene in the book. Kasey should be less nervous and heavily turned on instead. No wonder the mile-high club exists.

Phil starts explaining how to start the aircraft. I had no idea it was so complicated. Next time I fly I'm going to hug my pilot after. I've heard people say it's like driving a car. Umm . . . No, it's not.

"You always want to make sure you're lined up on the centerline." He motions outward to look down the runway.

"Right now you're going to apply full power. Then, at the

same time you're going to add some right rudder."

He's pointing to stuff and I can hear Fisher acknowledging him in my ears. I can't believe we're going to do this.

"You want to make sure the engine gauges are normal. That typically means in the green range. Now apply backpressure to the nose. Not fast and not slow. Nice and easy . . ."

I grip the armrests as we leave the ground.

"Woohoo!" Fisher laughs.

After a few minutes, Fisher glances back at me. "Are you enjoying our first date?"

"You could have just bought me ice cream, you know."

"If you want ice cream, you got it. We'll have to squeeze it between all the other stuff I have planned."

There's more? Mentally I race through the pages of the book. What in hell comes next?

I watch as Fisher takes a picnic basket out of his trunk. It's a little after seven and the sun is just starting to set. It's getting a little chilly. I'm glad I brought a coat.

"How about over here?" he asks, pointing to the grass a few feet from his Jeep.

He places the basket on the ground and starts to unfold a blanket. I rush over to help him lay it out on the ground.

"Are you hungry?" he asks, glancing at his phone.

"I'm always hungry. Plus, I'm really curious what you brought."

He smiles. "In your story, Penn takes her for Italian. I didn't think it would hold up in a basket very well, so I improvised." He gazes down at his phone once more.

"Am I keeping you from something?"

"No, I'm just waiting for . . . Oh, there he is." He dashes off toward an approaching van. I lean back to read the writing on the side. Luigi's.

He runs up to the driver's window and hands him some cash. The driver hands him a very large bag.

"Did you buy one of everything?" I ask as he returns.

"I got a variety because I didn't know what you'd like." He places the bag next to me on the ground, opens the basket, and removes packs of ice from inside along with a bottle of wine and two glasses. I peek into the paper bag. It smells amazing.

"Go ahead," he says, motioning with his head as he starts uncorking the bottle.

I pull out three containers and put them on the blanket. The first one is lasagna, the second is mushroom ravioli, and the third is chicken fettucine alfredo. I hear a pop and Fisher hands me a glass of wine. He pours himself a glass and proceeds to take out two plates, silverware, and napkins.

I'm in awe.

"Have anything you want. I hope I chose well."

"You chose very well, but before we eat, we need to talk."

"Your nose is doing that little twitching thing it does when you're serious. Lay it on me."

I rub my nose. What twitch? He takes a sip of his wine and watches me closely. "You need to stop this."

"Stop what?" he asks.

"All of it. Following my book. Trying to make it real. It's amazing and unbelievably sweet, but it has to be costing you a fortune."

"Don't worry about that."

"I am worried and it's not necessary."

He sighs. "Let me ask you a question. All this stuff you've written about . . . the concert at the office, the dress and dinner, the being taken away for the night . . . is that based on actual events or is it all fantasy?"

"It's fantasy. Everyone knows that stuff never really happens. It's why so many women read books about it. It's nice to think that it could happen, but it's never happened for me or anyone I know."

"That's the thing, Greer. It should be happening for you. You deserve all this and more."

My head tilts to the side as I regard him. "You don't know me. How do you know what I deserve?"

He opens the container of lasagna and starts putting some on my plate. I watch him do the same with the other two. He opens the bag and hands me a breadstick. "Butter or no butter?"

I take it from him and get up on my knees. "If I seem the least bit unappreciative, I'm sorry. Honestly, it's been amazing. This whole day. But I don't expect any of it."

"And that's exactly why you deserve it."

"Fisher . . ." I sigh in frustration.

"Your dinner's getting cold. Let's eat and watch the sunset." He snaps his fingers and pulls out a jar candle. He feels around in his pocket and pulls out a lighter.

"Is there anything you didn't think of?" I ask, taking a large bite of my breadstick.

"Probably. Good thing your stories are so descriptive. Penn's got game."

"Penn isn't real."

"I need to live up to your standards."

"Dear God, Fisher! No, you don't."

He takes a big bite of ravioli and moans lightly. "Did you try this yet?" He holds out a fork of ravioli to me and I eat it. I nod in approval as I chew.

He puts another on his fork and hands it to me. Before I take another bite I ask, "Did you really read the whole book?" I'm guessing he must have to know what he knows.

"Twice. The second time I placed tabs at the parts I thought I should remember."

"Like what?"

"One of my favorites is the beach." He winks and my face heats.

"I'm sorry I asked."

"Did I really make your toes curl?"

"Oh my God! Stop."

"What? I need to remember what I did right in case I get the chance to do it again."

I put my fingers in my ears and stare at the checkered pattern on the blanket, silently willing him to drop it.

"I also liked the part where you said you'd follow me anywhere."

I shake my head and start to hum lightly.

"And that whole thing you said yesterday about never thinking about me? Come on. The whole book is about me."

I hum louder. I can still hear him laugh, but he doesn't need to know that.

"And when you said you thought I was a professional kisser? Man, what an ego boost that was."

Jumping up from the blanket, I shout, "Okay! You made your point. But I didn't think all those things. I just wrote them like that because we writers need to embellish things to make them better than they are. Like I said . . . fantasy."

He takes another sip of wine. I can tell he's amused. He pushes up from the ground and steps over to me. My stomach flips when he brushes a piece of hair away from my eyes. "Prove it."

I place my hands on my hips. "And how would I do that?"

"Let me kiss you. If you seriously feel nothing, I'll never do it again."

"I don't need to prove anything to you!"

He smiles. "Okay, I'll just go on thinking I was right."

"You're an asshole."

"I'm a *right* asshole."

"You're totally wrong, but you can just go ahead and think whatever you want. I don't care."

He shrugs and sits back down, leaving me standing there. He takes a bite of the lasagna. "So good. You should eat it while it's warm."

"You're not right, you know. I thought you were okay, but I made up the rest just like I made up the whole book."

"Okay. I believe you."

"No, you don't!"

"Really, Greer. If you say you felt nothing then I believe you. You don't have to prove anything." He winks at me again and grins cockily.

My teeth and fists clench at the same time. "Stand up."

"I'm eating right now. Maybe later."

"Dammit, Fisher, stand up right now so I can prove it to you!"

"Nah. I'm good."

"Goddammit! Kiss me!"

His eyes darken as he places his plate on the blanket, stands, and slowly walks over to me. He lightly touches my cheek with his fingertips. There's no more humor in his expression. "You want me to kiss you?"

"Just do it already!" I roll my eyes.

He grins before he gently places his mouth against mine. I'm determined to feel nothing. His tongue softly pushes past my lips and he deepens the kiss. I repeat the word "nothing" over and over in my mind, but my body betrays me and I find myself kissing him back.

The tension leaves my shoulders. He places his hand on my hip and gently pulls me closer to him. I forgot just how good this feels. *No. No, it sucks. It's not good. Oh shit, yes, it is.*

As he quickly breaks our connection, I slightly stammer and sway. He's not smiling. He's just staring into my eyes. "For the record, if by chance I am a good kisser, it's only because you have the most perfect mouth I've ever seen."

I have nothing to say and I think he knows why.

"How about we call that a draw? If I had written about my thoughts from the beach it would have ended up in the porn section. And as much as I'd love to stand here kissing you all night, it's getting dark, and I promised you a meal."

We return to the blanket and eat in silence, stealing occasional glances and smiles at each other. A plane takes off in the distance and as it tips its wings into the air, I feel the scales slowly start to tip more and more in his favor. But then, I remember he's being who he thinks I want him to be. Is this real or just another story in a book? It's time I find out for sure.

CHAPTER 12

Even though I'm only supposed to be coming in three times a week, I've been here almost every day. When I'm at home alone I get stir-crazy.

I spent most of the morning going over more details of my date with Fisher with Luna even though I called her immediately when I got in the car last night. He texted me last night after I left to make sure I got home safely, which scored him major bonus points, but I haven't heard from him yet today. It might be bothering me a little.

I have no idea how this dating shit is supposed to work. Assuming that's what I'm doing. I was never much of a dater before Ollie and I haven't had a date in years.

Should I text him? Is that too eager? Do I wait for him to text me? Do I call? Ugh, this sucks. I'd hate to be a teenager in this day and age. Every time my phone has pinged today I couldn't look at it fast enough. It's never been him.

I guess I shouldn't worry why I haven't heard from him. Fisher mentioned he'd be filming all day today before I left last night. I was glad I drove myself to the airport. If he had had to take me home, it would have been a lot harder to say goodbye.

But still, I haven't been able to stop thinking about him all day. If I can't figure out how to stop thinking about him, I may cave and text him or something stupid. Who am I kidding? I'm writing a book where he's the star. Not thinking about him is impossible.

As I wash my hands in the bathroom, I decide on "hope you're having a good day." That's safe, right? I tell myself that if I get back to my desk and I haven't heard from him, I'm totally going to text him that little phrase. It's harmless enough.

As I walk back to my office, I start doubting whether or not I should. Jeez, this is hard. I read somewhere once that men are natural pursuers. If a guy is not actively trying to get you then he's just not that into you. The thought has me considering watching the movie "He's Just Not That Into You" when I get home. Maybe it'll give me some pointers.

Brenna perks up more than usual as I approach. "Hey. You got a call while you were gone."

"Oh, from who?"

She smiles. "That book guy. I saw him on YouTube! Yowza!"

"What? Fisher? He called the office?"

"Yeah, um, Luna was standing here when it came through. She said she'd talk to him." She glances down at the switchboard. "She's still on with him."

My heartbeat jumps into my neck. It's beating in time with an alarm clock warning.

As I start stiffly toward Luna's office I say a silent prayer that she's making idle chatter. Her office door isn't completely closed and I stop dead in my tracks when I hear her speaking. I lean my head against the doorframe to listen.

"And I'm glad to hear that. I just need you to know how important she is to me. She'd never tell you herself because she's too proud, but her ex did a number on her. I've never met a more emotional abusive man in my life. People might wonder why she's so untrusting, but if you'd been made to second-guess every decision you'd ever made for years, you'd know why."

Oh fuck. I close my eyes. Part of me wants to charge in there and tell her to shut it, but the other part of me is kind of glad she's explaining me to him. It's something I'm not good at doing and I feel bad that I've been so standoffish with him. I have major trust issues.

"And she has major trust issues. She's not only my best writer, she's also my best friend."

Aww, Luna. I almost sniffle.

"So if you hurt her in any way, shape, or form, I will hunt you down, put you in the trunk of my car, and drive you to an undisclosed location where I'll pull each and every one of your toenails off with a pair of tweezers. Understand?"

I sprint into her office, waving my hands in the air.

"No worries. Bye." She places the phone into the receiver. "Oh, hey. That was Patrick. He said he had to go. He only had a few minutes between takes."

"What the fuck? Why did you say that? He's probably scared to death now."

Luna smiles. "No, he's not. He was laughing."

"Laughing how?" I ask. "Like tee-hee nervous, I don't know how to respond to this lunatic laughing?"

"Luna-tic? Hey that's good. I always thought I was

named after the moon. Maybe it was a crazy person?"

I throw myself onto her couch and cover my face with my hands. "He's probably never going to call again."

"He was laughing like I was amusing. He told me not to worry. He said he liked you and his toenails too much to risk hurting either one of them. I like him. He's sharp."

"He said he liked me?" I ask, gazing at her through the small opening I made with my fingers.

"Duh. You didn't know that?"

"Why did he call the office? He has my cell."

Luna shrugs. "I don't know. All I know is he's at work. What's the plot of this new show?"

"I dunno. I never asked him." Now that I think about it, I haven't asked him a single question about himself ever. It's all been book talk. "What did he say before he hung up?"

"He said, 'Oh shoot, gotta go. Break's over.'"

"Not tell Greer I'll call later or anything?"

Luna shakes her head. Maybe she scared him off after all.

It's a little after eight when I return to my TV after getting ice cream from the kitchen. I'm not sure watching "He's Just Not That Into You" was the smartest decision I've ever made, but now that I'm halfway done, I'm not quitting.

This movie is making things so much worse. I relate to Ginnifer Goodwin's character on so many levels. I find myself talking to the TV. "Just be you, girl. Fuck him." I take another large spoonful of ice cream and let the spoon sit in my mouth, while I reach over and turn off the light next to the couch.

I hear my cell phone vibrating, but I don't see it. I've

pretty much had it sitting on my lap the whole night. Where the fuck did it go?

I jump from the couch in a rush as the vibrating continues. Where is it? I throw my blanket on the ground, toss the couch pillows to the floor, and panic when I can still hear the buzzing but can't see the phone. I press pause on the TV so I can hear better.

The sound is farther away than I thought it was. Suddenly, I think about the ice cream in the kitchen and I take off running, spoon still in my mouth. In my mind, the pillows are track hurdles and I'm jumping them like I'm in a race as I rush to the phone. I get to it in time to see Fisher's name pop up. I answer. "Hevvo?"

"Greer?"

I take the spoon from my mouth and whip it across the room.

"Hey? What's up?"

"Did I catch you at the gym? You sound out of breath."

I consider lying and saying yes to hide my embarrassment. Obviously, I don't need to be eating ice cream if I'm winded from running to the phone. "No, I'm good. How are you?"

"Tired. It's been a long day. Sorry this is the first I've spoken to you. My cell phone was out of reach all day during filming. I tried to call you at the office from a set phone, but you weren't available."

Millions of thoughts shoot through my head like bees rushing from a busted hive. Each one of them worse than the one before as I try to decide whether or not to mention I knew he'd talked to Luna.

"Did your boss tell you I spoke with her?"

The bees cease their buzzing and two boxes appear in my brain. One says yes, the other says no. I stare at them as I decide which one to check. "Yes?"

"That sounded like a question," he says with a light chuckle.

I walk back to the couch with the phone pressed to my ear. "That's because I'm not sure I should even admit to knowing her."

He laughs. "Did she tell you about it?"

"I kinda caught the last few seconds of it from the hall. I'm mortified. I'm so sorry."

"For what? She seems like a really good boss and friend."

"She means well, but I was a little worried she scared you away."

"Me? Aww, hell no. There's not a lot that can deter me when I've made up my mind about something."

"Oh." I grin. Sliding my legs underneath me, I suddenly feel like a schoolgirl talking to her crush. Lifting my eyes to the screen, I see Ginnifer Goodwin's face. I paused at a spot where she's crying. That's so not me. "How was your day? I never did ask you what you're working on."

"We just finished the pilot for a new show called 'Green.' It's about a woman who's envious of everything another woman has, so she tries to change her life around to be more like her. The idea is she's green with envy."

"That sound cool. What's your role?"

"I'm the other woman's boyfriend and the envious one is trying to steal me away."

"Oh . . ." I picture him kissing a lot of women on screen and I realize there is a reason he's a great kisser. He practices a lot.

"Hopefully it gets picked up. I like the idea of having a steady gig and being really close to a certain celebrity."

I swallow hard and my chest constricts. I bet his co-star is gorgeous. I immediately picture Olivia Wilde kissing him and I run the gamut of emotions. "So, you and your co-stars must be really close then, huh?"

"Not really. We just started filming last week. It's awkward having to do some of these scenes when you've barely shaken your co-star's hand."

"Awkward? You mean like lying naked with them and making out?"

He laughs lightly. "Oh, I see where this is going now. I should have known when you didn't react to my comment about being close to a celebrity. For the record, I was referring to you."

"Me? I'm not a celebrity."

"Is that why I saw them discussing your book on *Access Hollywood* yesterday?"

"They were? What?"

"It was a brief segment, but they said something about it being made into a movie."

"Oh, that little thing." I laugh as I wave him off in the air, even though he can't see me.

"Yeah, that. Congratulations, by the way. I can't even imagine how excited you must be."

"Thank you. They're still working on the script. I get to read it, but I'm not sure how open they'll be to my suggestions. Hopefully they try to stick to the book as much as possible. There's nothing worse for readers than watching their favorite book scene be mutilated on the big screen."

"I can imagine. I like this."

"What?"

"Us talking like this. This is the most you've ever said about yourself since I've met you."

I cringe. "Sorry. While my stories might be open books, I prefer my life to be as closed as possible."

"I understand. I just hope it means you might consider letting me in a little bit."

I pause because I don't know how to respond. What's appropriate here? Yes, welcome to my world. Explore all my nether regions? Or maybe, I'm not sure you'll like what you see in my folds, especially the crevices of fat. Or better yet, no, I don't know you enough to let you seep inside. I still haven't decided if you're sugar or poison.

He interjects before I decide which one to use. "There's no pressure. I'm not trying to rush anything. Although I'd be lying if I didn't have a particular chapter in mind."

"What chapter? Tell me." I rush over to my bookcase and grab *Book Boyfriend* off the shelf.

"No, no. I'm not ready to tell you yet. I wish I could see you sooner, but I'm scheduled on set all this week. Do you think you'd be open to phone dates until Saturday? Assuming you're free this Saturday night?"

"Hmm . . . I'll have to check my schedule. Um, yeah I'm free." I can't help but laugh. It's cute he thinks I have a life.

"Good. I miss your face."

I bite my lip. "I miss yours, too."

"I'd call that progress. I like that you miss me."

"Well, don't let it go to your head. I'm still not sure about you."

"That's okay. I'm a very patient man. The good things in life always take effort."

"Ha! You think I'm good? I'm actually a pain in the ass. Ask Luna." I instantly regret bringing her up.

"Luna seems fierce. I might be a little scared of her if I wasn't used to having strong women in my life. But next time she answers the phone for you, I'll make sure to ask her about all your bad qualities."

"Let's both pray she never does it again. I'm sorry for that. She really had no business talking to you that way."

"Don't be sorry. I appreciated it."

"Oh, you like the idea of being kidnapped, huh? You must be a sick pervert."

"You can kidnap me any time you want. And I think I'll wait a little while before I reveal all the sick, twisted things about me. Including what I'd be willing to do to you."

How do I respond to that? I visualize opening a locked door and a small cat scurrying out excitedly. She's been locked in there for ages. I decide it's time I let my inner kitty cat out to play. "I write sex for a living, Fisher. You'd have to really push the envelope to surprise me."

"Challenge accepted. Did it just get hot in here? I think I'd better go while I'm ahead. I need a cold shower."

"What's wrong? Am I too much for you?" Rrrarrr . . . I imagine my kitty claw pawing him in the air.

"Hell no, and if I were there right now, I'd move in a little closer."

"So move in a little closer."

"Are you in your bed?"

I glance around the room and stare at the dripping container of ice cream on my coffee table. "Yes," I lie.

"What are you wearing?"

Oh, this got dirty fast! I gaze down at my pink flannel

PJs. "A T-shirt and underwear." Flannels aren't hot.

"Maybe I should FaceTime you."

Oh shit. I think I have dried ice cream on my chin. "I think we're doing fine like this."

"So am I in the bed with you?"

"No. You just walked in the room."

"I walk in and see you in your bed in a T-shirt and underwear?"

"Yeah. What are you going to do about it?" I slide down so I can lie on my couch. Fuck, this is fun.

"I'm walking over to you right now and I'm taking off my shirt as I move."

"Uh-huh."

"When I reach you, I slowly run my fingers along your bare skin, from your calf up to that hot dragonfly tattoo on your thigh."

My body tingles all over. He noticed.

"Then I crawl on top of you and suck on your bottom lip."

"Uh-huh." My fingers begin to trail down my chest.

"I lift your shirt at the hem and slide my hand underneath it, pulling on your nipple with my fingertips."

"You're really good at this. Do you have a side job as a phone sex operator?" I ask through a giggle.

"Shh . . . tell me where your hands are."

"My hands are on your back, but I'm slowly sliding them down to your ass. You have a really nice ass."

"I like the way you're touching me. It's making me want more. My hand trails down your stomach to the edge of your underwear."

"Uh-huh . . ."

My phone beeps with another call. I lift it from my ear. In

big letters I see the only name that could make this conversation end. Mom.

"Oh shit, Fisher. You're not going to believe this, but my mom is calling on the other end. I'd ignore it, but she's one of those people who'll keep calling until I answer."

He laughs. "Cock-blocked by Mom. Go answer. Tell her all about me and my tight ass. I'll talk to you tomorrow."

"K. This was . . . fun."

"Yeah. It was. Good night."

"Good night."

As I switch lines I suddenly feel like I got caught having sex in church. This call with my mom is about to be breathy and fifty shades of awkward. I miss him already. Uh-oh, that can't be good.

CHAPTER 13

I got to third base with Fisher last night. On the phone.

Our daily phone calls get hotter every time we talk. They never start out that way. We usually go through our days and then I find out a little something more about him.

So far I know he was a really good student in high school but didn't have a lot of friends until he blossomed in his senior year. He was tall for his age when he was younger, but then he seemed to stop growing for a while. Then his acne cleared up, he grew six inches, and he started working out. He suddenly got way more popular. He played basketball for his first two years of high school but then switched to theater when a girl he liked tried out for the school play. The thing with the girl didn't work out, but the acting did. He loved it and that's when he decided it was all he ever wanted to do.

I find myself blushing at work and everywhere else when I think of him. I may talk a good game, but the truth is, I haven't had a lot of sexual experience. I've only ever been with my ex-husband. I think we had good sex, but I have nothing to compare it to and that makes me a nervous wreck.

It's Saturday today and all I know is he's picking me up at seven. I already got a mani-pedi, but I can't decide what to wear. I need to look my best. I even started wearing a T-shirt and underwear to bed so I didn't feel like a liar. Last night, Fisher felt me up again for the first time since the beach.

I mean, I may have touched myself while he was talking, so it was kind of the same, but not really.

He was being secretive about where we were going, so I checked my book. At this point, Penn takes Kasey to a fancy restaurant he rented out for the night. Kasey gets all dressed up and a limo comes to get her. When she walks in, Penn is sitting at the piano and starts to play. He sings "Can't Help Falling in Love" and that night he admits he's in love with her.

I was a little worried Fisher was still following the book, but when he told me to dress casually, I'll admit I sighed in relief. I don't want to follow my book anymore. I want to get to know him for *him*, not the guy he thinks I want him to be.

The fact I get to wear jeans and he's picking me up himself makes me think I've finally gotten through to him.

I spent way too long getting ready. I finally settled on jeans and knee-high black boots, with a button-down black blouse. I'm going to wear a light cardigan-like sweater over it because these jeans are a little snug. If I eat too much, I may have to undo the top button and that wouldn't be attractive at all. Hopefully, the sweater will help me in case I need to hide. Glamorous I am not.

It's five after seven and I've been ready for forty-five minutes. I guess his being early at the airport was a one-time event. I start to worry he's not coming when there's a knock at my door.

Suddenly I'm more nervous than I've ever felt in my life. I'm confident on the phone but up close and personal is another story. On the phone, I can talk like I'm writing. In real life, in front of him, I feel like I have no words. Why is this guy so interested in me? It doesn't make sense. He could have any girl he wanted. Why me?

I open the door to a bouquet of red roses and a smiling, panty-dropping Patrick Fisher. He's wearing a white dress shirt, dark faded jeans, and a black suit coat. He looks like he stepped off a runway and I just walked out of Walmart.

His eyes say something very different. He stares at me like I look at a sale rack at Macy's. "Wow. You're beautiful."

I roll my eyes as I take the flowers from his hand and he steps inside. "Thank you for these. You didn't have to."

"I know I didn't have to. I wanted to. And why did you roll your eyes at me?"

"It's nothing. Come on in. Let me put these in water then we can go."

He follows me to the kitchen. "It's something or else it wouldn't have happened. Tell me. Is it the flowers?"

"No. They're perfect."

"Is it because I'm a few minutes late?"

"No. I usually wait for everyone. I'm perpetually early, so I've grown accustomed to it."

"Is it what I said?"

I sigh. "It's nothing. Can we drop it?"

He leans his back on the counter as I place the flowers in a vase and add water.

"You don't take compliments well, do you?"

"I don't believe compliments. Isn't that the same thing?"

He crosses his arms. "No. That's entirely different. Not

taking them well means it's hard for you to hear. Not believing them means you don't see what others see."

"Where are we going tonight?" I ask as I put the vase on my table.

His lip curls up on the side as he regards me. He shakes his head lightly then straightens his posture. "It's a surprise. Shall we go?"

"What's with all the surprises?" I ask as he opens his car door for me. "Why not just tell me?"

He closes my door and jogs around to his side, sliding in the seat and pressing a button to start the car. "A friend of mine owns a bar downtown. I heard they have amazing food and great entertainment. I thought we'd pop in. Is that okay?"

I can't help but smile. "Sounds great." I'm so glad he's finally being himself. Maybe I can relax after all.

It's a forty-minute drive to the bar. I find out Fisher has very diverse taste in music. He introduces me to a country band named Old Dominion and a song called "Snapback," which I surprisingly like immediately. In the next song we listen to "Walk on Water" by Thirty Seconds to Mars. It's constant variety. He keeps me on my toes. He's hard to pin down.

After we get on the highway, Fisher opens his hand to me across the seat and continues to hold mine and drive one-handed. I'd be lying if I said I didn't like holding his hand. Ollie never did it. To me, it's like claiming someone, especially in public. It lets everyone know you're not just a random person, but rather someone important. I wonder if he'll still hold my hand when we get to the bar.

We drive around for a good ten minutes before we're able to find a spot to park. He offers to drop me off at the door, but there's no way I'm going in without him. He has no idea how socially awkward I can be. Whenever I go anywhere public by myself, I feel like I have a neon sign flashing above my head that says "No one wanted to come with me."

He places his hand on the small of my back and leads me through the door. It's rather dark, with a reddish glow all around. There's a stage up front with a microphone, but I don't see a band. Maybe they haven't set up yet.

As soon as we're inside, he takes my hand in his and leads me around tables to the bar. If I didn't know any better, I'd say I was walking on clouds. A girl in a short skirt and heels perks up when she sees Fisher. Her eyes move over to me and I feel as if my head was chopped off in her brain. I squeeze his hand a little tighter. That's right, bitches. This hottie is with me.

He releases my hand to shake the hand of a guy behind the bar. "Macy, this is Jeremy. He owns the place. He's a friend of my best friend growing up. We ran into each other a few weeks ago."

I hold out my hand to him and he shakes it. I'm really impressed that Fisher knows to introduce me as Macy. I only told him once that I never use my real name and he has honored my wishes ever since.

"Can I get you a drink?" Jeremy asks as he stacks glasses behind the bar.

"Captain Morgan and Coke in a tall glass with lime, please."

"I'll take what's on tap and start a tab for me."

"You got it, bro."

"Want to get a table?" Fisher asks as Jeremy delivers our drinks.

"Saved that one up front just like we discussed," Jeremy

says with a wink.

My Spidey senses start to tingle.

We walk over to a table but as I sit down, Fisher steps onto the stage. "Oh, fuck no."

He takes a swig of his beer and steps in front of the microphone, flipping it on with his finger. He taps it and the bar quiets down. I think I let out a small whimper, but I can't be sure.

"Hey there, everyone! Welcome to karaoke night at Jackson's! My good friend Jeremy Jackson over there was kind enough to let me kick things off tonight. I hope you're all half wasted already. I'll sound way better when you're drunk."

There's a few laughs and I awkwardly gaze around the room. There are at least fifty people that I can see. I'm going to vomit. What is he doing?

"I'm here on a date tonight with this beautiful woman in the front row. Everyone say hi to Macy."

There's a collective "Hi, Macy!" I lift my hand without turning around and slide down in my seat. I beg Fisher to stop with my eyes. I even mouth the word "No." He only smiles brighter. He removes his jacket and tosses it to me. I catch it and watch as he rolls the sleeves of his dress shirt. What is it about rolled sleeves that make every man that much hotter?

"This song is for you Macy. You might want to chug that drink."

It's then that I notice a small screen on the floor. Fisher nods to someone off to his right and a screen comes down on the side of the stage. I assume for the audience to see the words.

The music starts and I realize I'm back in my book. He just re-wrote the scene.

With the opening notes I know what he's singing. It's "Can't Help Falling in Love." *Dammit, Fisher. I thought we were done with this.*

He starts to sing and my frown turns upside down. I can't help it. He's not bad, but he's not great. No one in the crowd seems to care. His overabundance of confidence makes it enjoyable and fun. Before the chorus he announces, "If you know it, sing along."

The whole bar follows his lead and lifts their drinks in the air. His singing is drowned out as the bar shouts the lyrics along with him. I can't help but laugh as he finishes the song and takes a bow. The bar whoops and hollers like Adam Levine just finished a set. He hops down from the stage and bends down, planting a kiss on my cheek.

"Where's Amy Taylor?" the man on the side shouts. A girl takes the stage and sings another song. I guess there's a list of people waiting for their chance to perform. Who knew so many people were that confident?

He smiles as he sits across from me and lifts a menu. "I heard they have good wings."

"Oh no you don't. What in the hell? I thought I told you to stop."

"Stop what?"

"This stupid thing you have with following my book."

"I didn't rent the place or send a limo."

I sigh.

"And I can't play the piano for shit, so I improvised. Again."

How do I explain this to him? How can I get him to understand what I'm saying? Why is he so hot? My mind can't help but wander. I take a long swig of my drink and hope it kicks in to give me the confidence to figure this out.

Turning my head, I try to find the location of the bathrooms. Once I see them, I stand and curl my finger at him to follow me.

Once we round the corner, I push him up against the wall.

"I like where this is going already," he says, pulling me into him.

"What's your name?" I ask.

"Huh?"

"What's your name? Answer the question."

He seems confused. "I thought we were past introductions."

"Is your name Patrick Fisher or is it Penn Fitzgerald?"

He smirks. "My name is Patrick."

"Uh-huh. So why in the name of Elvis Presley do you insist upon re-enacting every scene from my book even though I've repeatedly asked you to stop?"

"Is Elvis Presley a new holy term I'm not aware of? Did he get canonized?"

"It's not a joke." I slide my hand around his collar and run my fingers through the hair on the nape of his neck. "I don't want you to be Penn. I'm not falling for him, I'm falling for you."

His lips part and I think I hear and feel him inhaling a breath. Did I overstep? I push off his chest and take a step back. "Anyway. Just cut it out."

He pulls my arm and I crash back into him. He bends his head down so his mouth is an inch from mine. He cups my cheek in his hand and his eyes search my face. He's doing that smoldering thing and now I can't breathe.

"I want to make your dreams come true. I want you to

have it all."

"What if I don't know what I want? What if I write what I think women want, but what we really want . . . what we need . . . is simply to be looked at the way you're looking at me right now?"

"Then that would be really easy."

"Will you promise me no more surprises? No more of this Penn stuff?"

He grits his teeth and hisses through them. "I'll agree on one condition. We stop *after* the next chapter."

As he presses his lips to mine. I mentally race through the chapters of my book. I gasp when I realize what comes next and he smiles. Oh hell no.

CHAPTER 14

It's a quiet drive back to my apartment. We stayed at the bar through wings and at least ten more karaoke songs. I think I ate slower than I ever have before. I tried to make the night last longer, but we had to leave eventually. Now that we're almost back to my place, I'm starting to have a slight panic attack.

What am I going to do? He had to have been joking, right? I mean, he can't actually want me to re-enact this chapter for him, can he?

We have been undressing each other on the phone for a week now, but just because Kasey had the confidence to let Penn watch her masturbate doesn't mean I can do it. Is that what he wants? He's almost exactly followed the book up until this point, and in a way, I guess he deserves this chapter for his effort. I could throw him a bone and give him the one scene he wants. But being naked while he watches from the door? I'm afraid I'd make a fool out of myself.

How did this work again? Kasey poured Penn a glass of

wine and ended up spilling it all over her dress. She excused herself to change and Penn followed her to the bedroom. He watched her undress. She realized he was standing in the doorway and decided to give him a show. Oh fuck! Why did I have to write that chapter?

Fisher pulls the car alongside my apartment building. Is he going to park the car? What is he doing?

"This has gone on long enough. You have to know I was joking. I would never, ever ask that of you."

I nod, but I can't look at him. I'm too embarrassed. I'm not afraid to talk about sex. I've sat on panels at conferences and discussed sex scenes at great length. I'm not a prude. But somehow, talking about it in front of a bunch of women is really different than talking about it with one very attractive man.

"Greer, please look at me."

I swing my head to face him. It might have looked effortless, but turning my head was as difficult as prying a piece of wood from a vice.

"What I said to you was crude and disrespectful." He places his hand over his heart. "Please accept my apology. I thought you'd know I was kidding, but you've grown more and more distant ever since I opened my stupid mouth. I don't want you to ever feel weird around me."

"It's just . . . well, I write a lot of stuff. I have a very vivid imagination. But I'm afraid my actual experience doesn't measure up to any of my characters."

"I think I finally understand how I've been making you feel. All this time you've been asking me to stop trying to be like Penn and I didn't listen because in my mind, I thought I was doing exactly what you wanted. But now . . . now that I even hinted at you being like Kasey, I want to take back every uncomfortable thing I've ever done or said. I'm truly sorry."

He's so incredibly sincere. I can tell he feels awful. I don't want him to feel bad. I just don't know how to explain my fear of letting him down.

"Can we please forget I said anything? Go inside, crawl into bed, and focus on me not being a jerk. I'll text you when I get home."

"You want to go?" I ask, suddenly sad the night could be coming to an end.

He turns his body in the seat to face me more directly. "Don't you want me to go?"

"Why would I want you to leave? It's only eleven. Unless you have to get up early for work tomorrow?"

"I don't have to be in until noon. Are you sure?"

"Sure I want you to come in and watch TV? Yes, I'm sure."

He smiles brightly. "Did I mention how much I love watching TV?"

"I have a really nice setup. You should park the car and come see it."

He seems relieved. Maybe he was just as nervous as I was. Nah. Look at him.

"Go inside. I'll park the car and be up in a few minutes."

I shut his car door and take the elevator to my floor. I start to text Luna. She'll know what to do. I type, "I need your help. It's an emergency," before I decide not to send it. I know what she's going to say. *You made the hottest man in the world watch TV instead of letting him watch you undress? What the fuck is wrong with you? You've been talking about taking his clothes off all week and now when he's in front of you, you're going to chicken out?*

She would be right. I unlock my door and walk inside. Placing my phone on the table, I lean my back on the door and try not to overthink everything.

A knock startles me out of my thoughts.

I open the door to Fisher, leaning one hand on the frame while the other hand holds his suit coat, draped over his shoulder. Did he pose this way or is this natural? He has to know how gorgeous he looks. Jesus Jones. "Right Here, Right Now" just took on a whole new meaning. And now I'm singing the song in my head.

"Come in, right now," I say on accident, briefly closing my eyes as I internally berate myself.

He quickly steps through the door. "I really like your place. It's a great neighborhood."

"Yeah, I used to have a house, but Oliver got that in the divorce." Ugh. Why did I say that?

"That really sucks. I'm sorry."

"*I'm* sorry. I don't know why I brought that up. Sometimes I rattle when I get nervous."

"Hey," he says, tossing his coat on my chair and taking my hand. "There's absolutely nothing to be nervous about. I'm only here to see your TV."

I point to the screen and he walks over to the couch. He's here to see my TV. My Tanned Vagina? Toned Viagrasaurus? Tubed Vaseline?

"It's a big one," he says, motioning to the television set.

"That's what she said." Oh my God. I didn't.

"Ha. I think that should have been my line."

"I'm sorry. Ugh. I have sex on my brain." I hit myself in the head.

He clears his throat and stuffs his hands in his pockets. "Should we turn it on? The TV I mean."

"Yes, please. See if you can find a church channel."

He laughs as he kicks off his shoes and flops down on the sofa.

"Do you want something to drink?" I ask.

"Sure, what do you have?"

I open the fridge. "I have water, a half-gallon of milk, Dr. Pepper, and oh, wine!"

"Dr. Pepper sounds great."

I close the fridge and imagine myself slamming my head in the door repeatedly. Of course he doesn't want wine, you twat. You just told him there'd be no re-enactments tonight. "Stupid, stupid, stupid."

"What did you say?"

Oh shit. I said that out loud. "Nothing. Just a second."

"I couldn't find mass for us to watch, but I did find CNN. That should be boring enough."

Handing him the glass and the can, he places them on a coaster on my table. I sit down on the opposite side of the couch and he smiles at me. He crosses his ankles as he places them on the table and extends his arm along the back of the couch. His sleeves are still rolled to his elbow, and that, along with his arm being outstretched, makes his shirt even tighter in all the right places.

I scratch my head and blankly stare at the screen. After a minute, I pick a piece of lint off my shirt. This show is not doing a great job of distracting me. I notice the remote next to his foot. "Let's see what else we can watch."

The next few seconds seem to happen in slow motion in my mind. I reach out to grab the remote as he leans forward to grab his drink. My hand hits his hand, just as he picks up the glass. The glass wobbles in his grip before it slips, the brown liquid jumping out of the glass in response. The evil syrup stops mid-air to laugh at me and let me know it will make sure I'm mortified tonight one way or another. It purposefully wins Olympic records for farthest splash as it leaps onto the crotch of his jeans. He gasps as the cold liquid invades his private sanctuary. I see my aunt Rose's face telling me to join the convent. I decide she was right.

And then time resumes its normal pace once again.

"Oh shit! I'm so sorry!" I run for the kitchen and quickly grab a dish towel.

He stands and I see the extent of my damage. I quickly take the towel and start dabbing the wet spot by his zipper.

"Um, why don't you let me get that?" he asks.

I continue to dab the area. "I'm so sorry, I was reaching for the remote and I didn't see you go for your drink."

"Greer . . ."

I kneel down next to him as I focus on drying his pants. I flip the rag over to a dry spot and reach up to place my hand on his ass, so I can apply pressure. I don't realize what I'm doing until I feel his jeans grow hard.

"Oh my God." I look up to see his lips pressed in a firm line. He's trying not to laugh.

And then I realize my hand is on his butt as I kneel next to his rock-hard dick. I immediately release him and hand him the towel as I stand. "Hi, my name is Greer. I'm an idiot. It's nice to meet you."

He laughs hardily as I sit down and hide my face in my hands.

"It's fine. Really."

"You're soaking wet."

"It's not too bad, I think you, uh, got most of it. How do I look?" he asks, turning to face me.

I peek out through my fingers and gaze at the wet bulge in his pants. "You look like you peed yourself."

"It'll dry."

His words give me an idea. "Take off your pants."

"What?"

"Take them off. I'll toss them in the dryer down the hall."

"Are you sure?"

"Yes, I'm sure." I stand and hold my hand out to him.

He shrugs and starts to take off his belt. He's halfway through the zipper when I realize I just asked him to get naked in my living room.

"Oh shit! Oh my God. Um, maybe you should go in the bathroom to do that."

"I'm not shy."

He tugs his jeans down his legs and I quickly turn my back to him.

"Here you go."

I hold out my hand behind me and I feel the material touch my fingers, but I can't grip it. I keep reaching for it, but I never get a hold of it. Looking over my shoulder briefly, I see he's laughing.

"Dammit, Fisher. Just give me your pants."

"Take them. I can't help it you're not reaching far enough."

I try and fail once more before I'm forced to turn around. He's standing in his boxers, package bulging. My eyes zero in on the bull's-eye before I force them to the ceiling.

"Go get a towel out of the bathroom. I'll be right back."

Walking down the hall, I toss them in the dryer and laugh. I make my way back to him and think, only me.

He's standing by the doorway when I enter the room. No towel. "Couldn't you find one?"

"You know, if you wanted to get me naked, all you had to do is ask."

I place my hands on my hips. "I didn't do that on purpose."

"Uh-huh."

"I swear I didn't!"

"Okay, I believe you." He shrugs.

"No, you don't. Fisher, I'm telling you, I did not get your pants wet just so you'd have to strip down."

"I know."

"I mean it!" I shout.

"I was just joking. I know it was an accident, but I had to tease you. It's kind of ironic, don't you think?"

And now I'm singing Alanis Morissette's "Ironic". His words hit home and I remember my story and how Kasey ends up wet, not Penn.

"Now where's that towel?" he asks.

"I'll get it. Just a second."

I walk down the hall toward the bathroom, stopping at the door and glancing back in Fisher's direction. He's great. I like him. I really like everything about him. Reaching for a towel on the shelf, something flips in my mind.

As I walk into my bedroom I feel different. I turn on the light in the closet, making sure to cast only a small glow in the room. Can I do this? Yes. Yes, I can.

I remove my sweater and toss it on the bed. I unzip my boots and remove them along with my jeans. I stand in the middle of my room in my shirt and underwear. It'll have to do.

I think about my rubbing the towel on his pants and how hard he became when I touched him. I sigh as I think about placing my hand inside his shorts on the beach. I focus on what it felt like to have his dick in my hands and watch his face as he came.

I drag my fingers over the material of my blouse and grab ahold of my breast, imagining his hands on me instead.

"Greer? Are you okay?"

I hear him call me and know it's only a matter of time before he comes looking for me. His footsteps down the hall are all the confirmation I need. I prop my leg up on the bed and close my eyes. I'm already wet and I want to do this for him. I want him.

I can sense his presence in the room, so I go ahead with my plan. I touch my nipples through my shirt and slowly trail my fingers down my stomach until I reach the edge of my underwear. Knowing he's watching turns me on more than I ever dreamed it would. I push my hand into my underwear and I hear him moan lightly. Rubbing gently, I turn slightly to make sure he can see that I'm touching myself.

Confidence runs through my veins. I open my eyes and look directly at him as I touch myself. His eyes are fixed on me and the bulge in his boxers has grown.

I slide my underwear down my legs and toss it in his direction. Then I sit on the bed and open my legs to him as I begin to rub all the right places.

He watches me intently for a few seconds and then unbuttons his shirt. Oh yes. Finally. I want to feel him inside me. He drops his shirt on the floor and takes one step toward me, when I hear the front door open and slam against the wall.

"Greer? Are you hurt? Where are you?"

I jump from my place on the bed and rush over to the bedroom door, closing it halfway.

"I'm fine, Luna! Don't come back here!"

I struggle to put my underwear on as she flies around the corner and down the hall.

"You can't send a text like that and then not answer your . . . Oh . . . Um . . . Hi, Fisher."

A normal person might turn around when they saw their best friend pulling up their underwear, but not Luna. She walks farther into the room and stares at Fisher now sitting on my bed.

She nods to him. "Hey, what's up?"

He points to his crotch and sighs.

I push Luna out the door as she says, "I can see that."

"What are you doing here?" I whisper shout.

"You texted me that you needed me. That it was an emergency. I tried calling you six times on my way over here. I don't even remember how I got here I was so worried. Be happy it was me who showed up and not the cops. I thought of calling them, or maybe Marcus. I was worried your alarm failed or something."

"I don't set the alarm anymore. There's no point. And I didn't think I sent that text. I was going to ask for advice, but then I changed my mind."

She rocks her hips. "I guess you figured out what I'd say from the looks of it."

"Can you please go? I really can't take any more humiliation tonight."

She mouths "Call me" as she walks backward to the door. Then she shakes her hands in the air and mouths, "So hot!"

right before she closes it behind her.

Fisher walks out of the bedroom wearing his shirt and a towel. "Aww, did she have to rush off like that?" he asks sarcastically.

"I'm so sorry!"

"For what? This has been one of the best nights of my life and more than I could have ever imagined."

Rubbing my forehead with the back of my hand, I realize I'm still in my underwear. I suddenly feel uncomfortable. What did I just do? He must sense my insecurity because he removes his towel and hands it to me.

"I bet my jeans are dry. I should probably get going."

I nod. "Give me a second."

As I pull on my jeans in my bedroom, I cringe. Another day in the life of Greer Hanson. How will I ever look him in the eye again?

CHAPTER 15

I spent Sunday in bed hiding under the covers and willing Saturday to be a dream. Fisher texted that he was tied up all day with filming and would talk to me tomorrow, but what *I heard* him say was, last night was awful and I need a day away from you to decide if I can put up with you anymore.

If I were a GIF right now, I'd be the first picture you see when you type in pathetic. It's Monday before 8:00 a.m. and I'm pouting my way into my office. All that's missing from this image is my kicking a rock on the way there. How did things go from YAY to NAY so quickly?

I put my bag on the floor and unlock my office door. I beat Brenna to the office. That's rare. I stand in the doorway and stare at my desk. I don't want to be here, but I don't want to be home either. This is going to be the longest Monday in history. Man, my life has changed over the last year.

I drop my bag on the floor and roll out my desk chair so I can sit in it. I wait for my laptop to whir to life and run my fingers through my hair. I just washed and brushed it before I left, yet there's a huge tangle. How in the hell does that happen? It's as if my individual hairs decided to hug each other on the way here. They must feel as bad as I do.

I click on my emails and see one from the production company. It's titled "First round script."

Holy crap. It's done!

I hear Brenna talking to Luna in the hall outside my door. I've been completely preoccupied with reading ever since I got the email.

"She was here before I was. I don't know. She hasn't said much. She looks like she hasn't slept."

I shout. "I can hear you!" as I make a comment next to a line I think could be better.

"Hey," Luna says as she walks in my office. "Are you writing?"

"Do I know something before you for once?"

"What?"

"The script is here."

"What?" She bolts alongside me and bends down to read the page I'm on. "How is it?"

I teeter my head back and forth. "All things considered, not bad. Not bad at all."

"Did they send me a copy?"

"I don't know. I didn't check."

"Okay, I'm on it." She rushes for the door and stops midway, spinning on her heel. "So . . . how did things go after I left Saturday night?"

I frown and lift my eyes in her direction briefly before refocusing them on the script.

"That bad?"

"He couldn't leave fast enough. I think he's done with me."

"No . . . no way! He doesn't strike me as a guy who gives up easily."

"Yeah, well, maybe he didn't like what he saw." I shrug.

"What did he say?" she asks, stepping toward me.

"Nothing really. I haven't talked to him. He said he was busy yesterday and has basically dropped off the face of the Earth."

"Did you text him?"

"And say what? Was my pussy not to your liking? Sorry my best friend showed up and mentioned how big your dick looked in your boxers."

She cringes. "Sorry about that. I was surprised."

"It's not your fault. I'm the one with slippery fingers. I honestly didn't think I sent that text. Maybe the phone company hates me too."

"Oh stop. Don't be a Debbie Downer."

"Maybe that'll be the title of my next book. I'll write a story about a pessimistic girl who sees negative everywhere she turns."

"Sounds like a real winner. You need to put positive vibes into the universe. If Fisher said he was busy, then he was probably just busy."

"Yep. I'm sure making out in front of camera is *hard* work. I put the emphasis on hard there. I don't know if you noticed."

"Yeah, I noticed. Do you want me to call him and apologize? See what he has to say?"

"God, no. Let him be. I have work to do. I don't have time for a relationship anyway."

"Think positive. I bet you'll hear from him soon."

I shrug. "I'm going to keep reading, okay?"

She nods then walks to the door. Out of the corner of my eye, I see her shoot me a pity pout. I refuse to acknowledge it. I don't care what anyone thinks. I have a job to do and that's what I'm going to focus on.

I've had a range of emotions today. I'm starting to think I have multiple personalities. One minute I feel confident and purposeful. The next, there are tears in my eyes and I want to crawl under my desk and rock myself. Being a water sign sucks. I hate that I care too much. Overthinking everything sucks even more. Why can't I be one of those people who doesn't give a shit?

After three hours of staring at my phone, I finally turned it off and put it in my purse in my drawer. Even if he texted me, I wouldn't see it. It gives me a sense of power to be too busy for him. But I keep finding reasons to open the drawer.

Is it dry in here? Gum would really do the trick. Did I bring my wallet to work? I'd better check. Dumbass. Is he that busy he can't even say good morning? People are only too busy for the things they don't care about. If he cared, he'd find a second to let me know. Men suck. All of them. They toy with our emotions, pulling us in just to push us away. Well, I'm done playing games. I'm too old for this shit.

Yanking the drawer open, I reach for my phone and plot the nasty text I'm going to send him. I turn it on and see I've missed five texts from him. Grinning from ear to ear as I read them, I realize what a complete basket case I've become. I was pissed and here the sweetie has been texting all along.

FISHER: *Hey, babe. Sorry I couldn't talk last night.*

We did fifteen takes on one scene. It was ridiculous.

I hope you had a good day.

Do you have any plans tomorrow night?

Call me when you get a chance.

Aww . . . he does care. I shake my head at myself and feel bad for hating on him. He didn't do anything other than work his ass off all day. I dial his number and spin in my chair to gaze out the window as it rings.

"Hi. How are you?" he asks.

"Good. How are you?"

"Tired. I didn't get home until two a.m. I'm sorry I didn't call."

"No biggie," I lie. "I knew you said you'd be busy."

"So you weren't worried?"

I pause. I could say no here. I could act like I have all the confidence in the world. Guys like confidence. Or, I could tell him I've been slamming drawers all day because I'm a mess. Hmm . . . decisions.

"You were worried. I can tell."

I shrug and then remember he can't see me on the phone. "Maybe a little. I figured you were upset with me for Saturday night."

"Ugh. Of course not. Why in the world would I be?"

"Because . . . Luna and . . . well . . . me."

"You? You mean you and your gorgeous body? I have spanking material for life."

I giggle and cover my mouth with my hand. "What are you doing right now?" I stammer and feel the need to clarify. "What I mean is are you getting ready for work or chilling? I didn't mean spanking the monkey."

He laughs. "I'm going to jump in the shower and head back to the set. But hey, are you free tomorrow night? They're having a little cast party, so our families can visit the set and see what we do. I'd love it if you'd come."

"Really? Wouldn't you rather have your mom or your brother?"

"They're all the way in Ohio. They'd never make it. But I would be honored if you'd come. Will you?"

How can I say no to him? "Sure. I'd love to."

"I'll text you the address. It starts at four, but you can come any time after if you're working."

"I think I'll skip out early."

"Great. Okay, I'll see you tomorrow. I'll try to text or call later, but there's a no phone rule while we're filming. The bigger stars break it all the time, but I can't risk being labeled. I can try to get to it on break, but those breaks are few and far between. I hope you understand."

"Me? Of course I do!" I wave my hand in the air like it's no big deal. The reality is that after a few hours, I'll probably start worrying needlessly again.

"Don't worry, okay? I'm crazy about you."

I bite my lip. "I'm crazy about you too."

"Good. Pretend I'm kissing you. I gotta go. Bye."

"Bye."

I end the call and swirl around in my chair like I'm floating. I don't remember ever having so many butterflies before in my life. It feels amazing. Tapping on my belly, I speak to them out loud. "Don't you leave me now. You make me so happy. You stay right there."

"Uh . . . everything okay?" Brenna asks.

I turn to see her staring at me.

"Are you pregnant?"

And this is how rumors begin.

CHAPTER 16

The first thing I notice are several trailers lined up along the side of a building. There's a big white tent with tons of people inside. I want to hurl. I didn't know what to wear, so I let Luna dress me. I stare down at my short skirt. I look like I'm trying too hard. Luna insisted I let all the other women see what I had to offer. Tugging down on my shirt in the back, I hope it will bring it up higher in the front to hide some cleavage. It's no use. The girls are on display. Ugh.

I park the car in the studio lot and text Fisher to let him know I'm here. Opening the door, I step outside and attempt to lengthen my skirt by pulling down on it. Suddenly tempted to leave, I wonder if I have time to run to the nearest Target for a new outfit.

"Hot damn."

Twirling to my left, I watch Fisher strut toward me. His walk reminds me of Channing Tatum in "Magic Mike." He's grabbing a hold of his lips as he shuffles his feet toward me with what I can only describe as swagger.

"Excuse me. I know this is a little forward, but would you like to climb back into your car and make out? Damn, you are fiiiinnnneee."

I close my eyes and shake my head, pulling on my shirt. "Is it too much? I let Luna dress me."

"Luna just became one of my favorite people in the world. Remind me to send her a fruit basket or something."

His arm swings around my waist and he pulls me tightly against his hard chest. "You look beautiful. I missed you."

My stomach does somersaults as I get a whiff of his cologne. He bends his head and kisses me below my ear. "Maybe we should skip this and go somewhere."

I snicker as I grab a hold of his tree trunk arms. "Wouldn't your crew wonder what happened to you?"

He sighs. "Probably. Thanks for coming. Are you ready to see what I do all day?"

"Sort of. You know how you always want me to open up and tell you more about myself? Well, I'm about to spill. I have major social anxiety. Usually, I'm okay once I get inside, but right before an event, I always feel like I'm going to pass out."

He listens intently as if I've somehow revealed the secret combination to a safe. "Hold on to me. If at any point it's too much, just squeeze my hand three times quickly and I'll get you out of there. Okay?"

I nod and he takes my hand as we walk. He points to a park. "We do a lot of the outdoor shots over there. There's a school up the street and we film there a lot on the weekends. I'm supposed to be a high school English teacher."

"You don't look like any teacher I've ever seen."

"Is that good or bad?"

"Let's just say I probably would have loved coming to school if I had a teacher who looked like you."

We enter the tent and I grip his arm with my free hand. He lets go of my hand and places his arm around my waist, pulling me snugly to his side. I feel safe and protected. It's a new feeling and one I could get used to.

"Macy, this is my director, Arthur Westbury. Arthur, this is my girlfriend, Macy Greer."

I can't help but do a double take at him. Did he just call me his girlfriend? I shake hands and smile at a lot of people over the next thirty minutes, but all I hear over and over in my head is him telling everyone I'm his. I don't know whether to jump for joy or be mad that he didn't ask me first.

All my thoughts go flying out the window when a gorgeous blonde shouts his name across the tent. Fisher immediately drops my hand and gasps. She rushes to him and he meets her halfway, picking her up and spinning her as he hugs her. Half the tent laughs as the other half seems to be questioning who she is, along with me.

"What are you doing here?" he asks excitedly.

"Do you think I'd miss a chance to see where my best friend works? So I had to drive a couple of hours . . . I still look fabulous, don't I?"

"As beautiful as ever."

Rubbing my forearms, I start to feel like everyone is watching me for a reaction. After all, he did just introduce me as his girlfriend a few minutes ago. Now it seems he's forgotten I exist. If he were next to me, I'd squeeze his hand three times, but since he's not, I decide to make him remember me.

"Fisher?" I question as I walk over to him and touch his arm.

He pulls his gaze away from her and smiles. "Macy, this is my best friend, Chloe. Chloe, this is Macy."

He fails to call me his girlfriend this time and if he thinks that little tidbit is lost on me, he's sadly mistaken. Chloe. I briefly remember him listing her as one of the few people he trusted while we were in Florida. I never gave her a second thought until now. My mistake.

I shake her soft hand. She smiles genuinely. Maybe she's a great person, but right now, I'm on edge and ready to fight for him.

"It's so nice to meet you. Fish talks about you all the time."

Fish? I cringe. "Oh? You two must talk a lot."

"Almost every day," she says, touching his arm. He smiles at her like he just found his favorite toy hidden under the bed.

"I can't believe you're here. Macy, do you mind if I introduce her to some people? Chloe and I used to model together when we were younger. She lives in L.A. now and I don't see her as much as I'd like anymore."

"No, not at all." I try my best to be polite even though I want to scream *don't leave me.* He seems so happy. Part of me is happy he's happy, but I can't help but feel jealous of the way she's taken a hold of his arm as they walk. I watch him introduce her to the same people he introduced to me. She's the "best friend." I'm the "girlfriend," although I wonder if Chloe knows that. She has the longest, most toned legs I've ever seen. I vow to start using the stairs.

She's wearing heels and walking on grass like it's nothing. I couldn't walk in those heels on hard pavement. Damn her for being so graceful and feminine. Her makeup is perfect.

It almost seems like she's not wearing any at all. I suddenly feel my pores crying out in agony for being smothered in foundation.

A man carrying a tray offers me a red punch, so I take it, praying it's laced with some kind of liquor. It tastes more like fruit punch than anything, but I try to pretend there's vodka in it so I can get through the day.

After a few minutes, they walk back over to me. Fisher kisses the side of my head and smiles down at me. It makes me feel a tiny bit better. I decide I need to find out more. "So, Chloe, how long have you two known each other?"

"Since we were . . . ten?" she asks, gazing at Fisher for confirmation. "We went to grade school together and became instant friends. Fish has always been my protector. He's fought off many a boy for me."

Fisher grins and shrugs as he looks at me.

"Uh-huh. He's very chivalrous."

"Then we moved to New York together while we went to school. We got a small apartment our junior year and never looked back." She smiles at him with pure adoration.

"You two lived together?"

She nods as she takes a glass of punch from a tray. "For four years in New York. He's been known to shack up at my place whenever he has work out this way. But I guess he didn't want the three-hour commute this time." She pouts lightly and he laughs.

"No way. I'm always late as it is. Macy can attest to that."

"I hope you don't mind, but I'm fangirling a little bit. I loved *Book Boyfriend*! It's my favorite book. I pimp you out to everyone I know."

"Aww, thanks, that so sweet of you to say."

"Fish talks about you nonstop. He told me about the flying lesson. He's such a romantic, isn't he?"

I nod and smile awkwardly at both of them as I down what's left of my punch. I want to say something like, *it's so sweet that he tells you everything.* Maybe even *did he mention I fondled my pussy in front of him the other day? Did you hear that part too?* And then I'd follow it up with *why haven't I heard a word about you? Are you his dirty little secret? You look like you might be a dirty girl.* But I bite my tongue. I'd seem as jealous as I feel and that would be very bad.

What reason would he have for keeping her a secret? They talk every day? You'd think them living together for years might have come up when he was giving me his history. But no, not a word. Why is that? Did they date?

"In a few minutes we're going to tour the set. I'm really excited for you both to see it."

Another gorgeous woman taps him on the shoulder. He turns and hugs her. "Macy, Chloe, this is my co-star Ireland Moore."

Chloe offers her hand first.

"Cute shoes," Ireland says with a smile. "Where did you get them?"

"Girl, I found them on sale at Filene's Rack. Do you believe I only paid six hundred for them?"

"That's a steal. We should go shopping together. I could use a friend with an eye for fashion like me."

"I'm totally down."

Oh goody. Bestie and work wife are bonding in front of my eyes.

"Hi, Macy, it's nice to meet you."

I smile awkwardly and that ends our interaction.

"Well, I should get back to the hubby," she says, taking a step back. She points her fingers from her eyes outward to Fisher. "I'll see *you* later."

I sigh in relief checking her potential threat off the list. Thank God she's married. Not that it means much anymore in today's world.

Chloe leans over to Fisher. "She's so nice."

"I know, right?" he responds. "I got really lucky to work with such a great cast."

The producer announces the start of the tour. Chloe grabs a hold of Fisher's arm, claiming him before I even get a chance to get near him.

Fisher holds his other hand out to me and I take it like a person who just won second place.

As we walk through the set, Fisher beams with pride. He glances at me from time to time to gauge my reaction, but he's mostly distracted by Chloe and her constant questions.

There's a small dinner after the tour and I decide it's the perfect time to excuse myself. "Hey," I say, pulling on Fisher's arm. "I'm going to take off."

"What? Why?"

"I have a lot of work to do and I think you could use some time catching up with Chloe."

He eyes me skeptically. "Okay, but can't you at least stay and eat?"

"I'd love to, but I'm not hungry."

He frowns.

"I'll talk to you later. Chloe, it was nice meeting you."

"Are you going? I was hoping we could hang out after this and get to know each other."

"Work . . ." I sigh, raising my hands in the air and rolling my eyes like I'm the busiest woman on the planet.

"Let me walk you to your car."

"No, you stay. I'll be fine. Thanks for inviting me. It was great."

I turn and quickly walk away before he has a chance to say another word. I can hear Luna's voice in my head telling me to fight for him, but it's not who I am. Looking back briefly, I notice Chloe has her hand cupped to Fisher's ear. He's listening to her and staring at me.

The tears prick my eyes. She's the type of girl he belongs with, not me.

Fumbling with my keys, I drop them on the ground. A masculine hand reaches for them. I gaze up as Fisher picks them up and hands them to me.

"What's going on? Talk to me."

My lips tremble and I desperately try to pull myself together.

"Did I leave you for too long? I'm so sorry. I know this was hard for you."

I shake my head and play with my keys in my hand.

"Then what's wrong? Do you really have a lot of work or is something else going on?"

"I got the script yesterday and they really need my edits."

He nods and crosses his arms. His eyes bore a hole into my brain as he tries to read my mind. "Okay, but you still need to eat."

"I'll be fine. As you can see, I have storage."

He sighs and pulls my arm until I'm against him.

"You do not have storage. You're perfect."

"Not as perfect as Chloe."

He takes a step back to see my face. "Is that what this is

132

about? She told me to go after you to reassure you."

"Aww, isn't she sweet." My sticky sarcasm makes him smirk.

"She's a good person. I'd really like for her to get to know you better."

"Why? She seems to know everything about me, yet you never once mentioned her to me. You tell her everything?"

"Not *everything*. Chloe and I have a weird relationship. She can be really needy. She's not proud of it, but it stems from years of bullying. Her self-esteem is almost non-existent."

"Could have fooled me."

"Are you jealous?"

"No."

"Seriously, are you worried about her?"

"No. Why would I be? After all, you introduced me as your girlfriend to everyone *except* her. Speaking of that, don't you think we should have discussed what was going on with us before you announced it to everyone else?"

His eyebrows lift in amazement and he raises his hands in the air as if to shield himself from my sudden anger. "Whoa . . . let me get this straight. You're mad because I didn't call you my girlfriend to Chloe *and* you're mad because I called you my girlfriend to everyone else?"

I toy with my keys once more as I realize how ridiculous it sounds. "Yes?" I gaze up at him through my lashes and wince. "I'm sorry, okay? I just started feeling like a third wheel."

"Babe, you are the main wheel. The only wheel, if you ask me. I didn't realize I didn't call you my girlfriend when I introduced you. I was shocked to see her. It was inconsiderate of me."

"No, it's fine. I'm just . . . I don't know . . . feeling insecure, I guess."

He grabs a hold of me and pulls me against his chest. "There's not a thing for you to worry about. I promise."

"Okay." I try to sound confident as I grip his shoulders and inhale his scent like it's the last time.

He pushes me back to study me. "Please come back and eat with us. It would mean a lot to me."

I don't know what to do. I want to stay, but I also want to go.

He stares at me while I try to decide. "Chloe told me that when I ran after you, I should tell you more about her."

"Like what?" I ask.

"It's a long story."

"Okay . . ." I say, watching him glance back to the tent. He rubs his hand along the back of his neck.

"What? Just say it." I mentally prepare myself to hear they dated.

"Oh . . . let's start off with the fact that when I first met her, her name was Joey. And . . . she was a guy."

"What did you say?"

CHAPTER 17

The waitress brings us our drinks and we toast to Fisher and his amazing acting talent.

After Fisher's little revelation in the parking lot, I decided to return to dinner with him. He told me it was Chloe's story to tell, but that she gave him permission to reveal that little tidbit so I'd feel less concerned about her. She made a joke about not being able to help the fact she was more woman than half of the women in the tent. It made me laugh and I felt awful for jumping to conclusions.

We ate dinner and went to a bar nearby for drinks. Chloe said she needed more than punch to get through the seedy details of her life.

"I think Fish knew I was different from the minute I transferred into his grade school. I was always hanging out with the girls rather than the boys. One day, I came to school with nail polish and this boy named Todd was making fun of me. Fish stepped in and stood up for me. He told them he liked the polish and might even wear it to school tomorrow. I remember him puffing out his chest and saying, 'What are you gonna do about that?' He was the biggest kid in class and that outweighed his awkwardness, so they backed off."

I gaze over at him lovingly. I didn't know it was possible to like him more.

"We became fast friends. I played kick ball terribly and he got hooked on a soap opera I watched with my mom after school. He was always there when I needed him. To be honest, I wouldn't be here today without him. I went through a really dark period when I didn't want to live anymore."

I swallow hard. I feel so bad for her.

"But you made it," Fisher says, smiling.

"Yes, I did. After we'd spent some time living in New York, I sat Fisher down to tell him I'd decided to start crossdressing. I was so afraid he'd be shocked to find out I was gay. I'll never forget his reaction."

Fisher smirks as he takes a sip of his beer.

"He was like, 'Um, yeah?' I almost fell over. He said he'd known that for years. He asked if I just figured it out."

I place my hand on his knee under the table and squeeze it gently. He glances over at me and winks.

"You were always my friend. That wasn't going to change. I didn't and don't care what your name is or how you dress. You're still the same person where it counts. Inside."

Chloe fans her face to hold back the tears and I feel them gather in my eyes as well. Fisher shakes his head at us and takes a long swig from his beer.

"Anyway, long story short, I modeled as Joey during the day and hung out as Chloe at night until one day I decided I liked being Chloe more than Joey. I saved up the money to get these bodacious tatas and the rest is history."

"So did you do the surgery and everything?" I ask.

She points downward and I nod.

"No. I looked into it, but I just couldn't bring myself to go under the knife. So basically I have boobs and a package."

I stare down at my drink for a moment and try to plan what I want to say. "I want to apologize for the way I behaved when we met. I felt a little threatened by you."

"Doll, that's the biggest compliment you could ever give me. I'd feel threatened by me too," she says with a laugh. "Fisher is like a brother to me. Even though he turned out to be a fine piece of ass, I can't look at him without seeing a sibling. It's gross."

Fisher laughs. "It's true. I disgust her."

"Do you feel better?" Chloe asks.

"Yes. So much. Thank you for being brave enough to tell me your story. I'm glad you have Fisher in your life. He's a good man."

Fisher's hand settles on top of mine.

"Yes, he is. Now how about a shot? We need to get this party started."

Fisher had too much to drink. Chloe, on the other hand, can handle her liquor like no one I've ever seen. She wasn't even tipsy. I'm glad I stopped after the second shot. I insisted I could handle him when she helped me get him to my car. I hugged her before I left. I'm glad she's understanding. She really is special. I can see why Fisher cares about her.

As I drive him back to his place, I can't help but stare at his face while he sleeps.

He's just as beautiful on the inside as he is on the outside. I don't know what's happening to me, but my heart wants to leap out of my chest. I check his GPS and follow the directions on his phone to get him "home." We pull into a motel lot and I feel bad when I see where he's living. It's a nice place, but it certainly doesn't feel like a home. I guess he's used to living here and there all the time when he's working. I almost wish I'd brought him back to my place to sleep it off.

"Fisher, we're here," I say, shaking his arm.

He jumps a bit when I nudge him but smiles when he sees my face. He leans across his seat and attempts to place his head in my lap.

"Oh, boy."

I reposition him so I can slide out of the car. Opening the passenger side, he tries to reach his arms out to me. He laughs when the seatbelt prevents him from moving and he touches it like he isn't sure how it works.

Squatting down next to him, I try to think how I should get him inside. I feel around on his jeans until I think I sense keys. Then I try to slide my hand in his pocket to retrieve them.

"Well, hi there," he says, sniffing my hair. "If you're going to feel me up I think we should go inside first. The parking lot is kinda kinky."

"I'm trying to get your keys, smart-ass." I unbuckle his seat belt and he lifts his hips so I can reach them.

"Oooh," he says in a sexy voice. "I like your hands in my pockets."

I laugh as I try to figure out which room is his. The key says Room 221. It would have to be up the stairs. Figures. "Sweetie, can you walk if I help you?"

He opens his eyes and smiles at me. "Huh?"

I reach over him to get my purse and place it over my head, propping it on my waist. "Okay, lean into me. We're going up the stairs."

It's a slow process, but I manage to get him standing. He's wobbly, but he's walking with his arm around my neck. It takes forever to get him up the first three. He's funny when he's drunk. He asks me if he can sit for a minute. When I tell him no, he pulls his lip down with his finger until he's pouting. We make it up three more before he announces, "Wait . . . I got this."

He straightens his posture and places his hands in the air. He hops up the last two steps without me and turns around proudly.

"Good job."

He tries to bow but stumbles. I rush over to him and he leans on me as I unlock his door. "You're hot, you know that?" he slurs.

I grin as I help him over to the bed. I close the door behind me and then fumble for a light switch. As light permeates the small room, I hear shuffling behind me. Fisher has removed his shoes and pants and seems to be caught up in his shirt.

I laugh and lean back against the door to watch him.

"Uh-oh," he says like a little boy. As I stare at his muscular thighs and sculpted abs, I can say beyond a shadow of a doubt, he's not a boy. He's *all* man. "Let me help you." His hands flop to his sides as I try to get his shirt off his head. He failed to unbutton it first, so I have to reach inside to get to the buttons. "How did you do this?"

Even though he can't see, his hands seem to have no

trouble finding my ass. I jump lightly when he squeezes my butt through my skirt.

"I wanna bite that." He moans as he squeezes harder.

I manage to get to his button inside his shirt and lift it off his head.

"Hey," he says when he sees me.

"Hey yourself. You're very touchy-feely when you're drunk," I tell him as he places his face on my stomach.

"You smell so good." He rubs his lips against my shirt and I almost stop breathing. Between him being almost naked, his hands on my ass, and his mouth so near my breasts I almost want to pretend he's not drunk and have my way with him.

His fingers find the zipper of my skirt and he starts to pull it down.

"Mmm . . ." I gaze at the heavens and pray for strength as I reach behind my back to stop him. "You're drunk."

"Uh-huh. You're hot. Did I say that already?"

"Yes, and thank you. But, you need to stop trying to undress me." I swat his hand from my zipper and he immediately starts to tug at my shirt. His hand makes its way under my shirt and he touches my breast.

"Let me kiss those," he whispers into my stomach.

Why did he have to get drunk? I want this to be sober Fisher right now. I feel like I should be curling my fake mustache in my fingers as I contemplate taking advantage of him. "No. You can't. Not like this."

"But, baby. I want you." His hot breath on my stomach sends ripples through my spine.

"I want you too, but only when I'm sure you'll remember in the morning." I step out of his grasp and he reaches for me in the air. I pull back the covers and fluff his pillow. "Lie down."

He scoots up on the bed until I can pull the covers down farther and as he lies back he grabs my arms and pulls me with him. "You want tops or bottoms?"

I laugh as I try to push off him. He's strong. "You need to sleep."

"I don't wanna sleep. I wanna taste your pussy."

I kiss his cheek. "Another day."

"No, now." He smirks and his perfect white teeth glisten. I kiss his lips because I can't help myself and he pulls me over to the side of the bed. He presses his lips to mine as his tongue invades my mouth. His hand cups my breast as he starts to un-button my shirt.

"Fisher, please stop. You're too drunk."

He pauses and gazes into my eyes. "Don't say no. I want to be with you." His forehead creases and his words get breathy. "Please stay with me." He's begging and it's so, so hot.

"I'll tell you what? I'll stay here with you tonight, but you have to go to sleep. Deal?"

"How about I sleep after I make love to you?" He kisses and licks my neck.

"No, you get to sleep next to me. No sex. Not until you're sober."

He nods in defeat and snuggles his face into the crook of my neck. A few seconds later, he's snoring lightly. His leg is draped over me and my hand is trapped underneath him. I try to move, but he's dead weight. I guess I should have thought this through a little better. Now what do I do?

CHAPTER 18

The sound of a flushing toilet startles me awake. I'm lying on my stomach, fully dressed and on top of the covers. Fisher isn't in the bed. It's dark in the room, but I can see a little from the streetlight shining through the curtains as well as from the light under the bathroom door. I rub my eyes. I must have fallen asleep.

"Hey," he says as he walks back toward the bed.

I push up into a sitting position, still rubbing my eyes.

"Sorry about that," he says shyly. "Are you okay?"

I nod. "You were cute."

He lies down next to me and pulls the covers over his legs and waist. "That's not how I remember it."

"I guess I should go. What time is it?"

"It's 3:00 a.m. I don't want you driving home this late. Will you stay? I promise to behave myself."

I smile and nod. "Yeah, I'll stay. Do you mind if I borrow a shirt?"

"Take anything you want. Top drawer." He tightens his

grip on his pillow, pushing it into a ball under his head.

I pull out the first shirt on top and go into the bathroom to change. After I pee, I take a look in the mirror. My makeup is smudged all over my face. I look like a whore from eighteenth century France.

I do my best to wash my face and change out of my clothes. I'm thankful his T-shirt is too big for me and covers enough to make me feel okay about walking back to him.

I place my clothes on the chair and walk back to the bed. His eyes are closed. I do my best to carefully pull back the covers on my side and he stirs awake. Noticing what I'm trying to do, he reaches over and helps me pull them back. I slide inside and in an instant I feel the heat of his body next to me. He's so warm.

"Your feet are cold," he whispers as he pulls me closer.

"I know. They always are."

"That's good to know." He's groggy and adorable.

He spoons me from behind. His warm breath fans my hair and I smile as I close my eyes. There's nowhere else I'd rather be.

I squint as I open my eyes to daylight. Fisher isn't in bed and I'm sad. I must have been sleeping harder than usual.

I roll over as he steps out of the bathroom wearing jeans and no shirt. By the steam in the air I can tell he's freshly showered. He's brushing his teeth, but it doesn't stop him from smiling at me. "G' morning."

"Hi."

He spits in the sink and walks over to me, sitting on the

edge of the bed. "Did you sleep okay?"

I nod.

"You aren't a morning person, are you?"

"No, but apparently you are."

He smiles. "Coffee?"

"Yes, please. What time is it?" I sit up and he hands me a cup.

"It's a little after six. I have to be on set by seven."

"Oh, okay. I'll get up and drive you." I slide my legs out the side of the bed and remember I'm only wearing his shirt and my underwear when the cold air hits my legs.

"No, I can Uber. I'm sure you need to get to work too."

I nod and slide back under the covers.

He watches me briefly and then walks over to the closet and starts putting on a button-down shirt. "Sorry I got so drunk last night."

I smile. "It was interesting."

"I came on pretty strong, huh?"

"You were hard to resist."

"Oh yeah?" He slides onto the bed and over to me. "Then why did you?"

"Because I wanted you to remember our first time."

"I remember everything from last night."

"Okay, I wanted you to be fully present."

"Hmm . . . you may have me on that one. But it was still fun. Thank you for staying. It was nice waking up to you."

He's doing that smoldering thing again and I want to kiss him, but I'm certain my morning breath would wilt his eyeballs. I smile and sip my coffee. "So, there's this thing on Saturday."

"What thing?" he asks as he puts on his socks.

"I'm a big supporter of this charity group that raises money for autism awareness. Anyway, once a year, they have a benefit gala and auction. It's this Saturday. I usually go alone every year, but I was wondering—"

"I'm in."

"What makes you think I was going to ask you to go with me?"

"Weren't you?"

"Well, yes, but—"

"Then I'm in. What time does it start?"

"Seven."

He pulls out his phone and starts flipping through emails. "Shit. Well, I'm working that day, but I should be done by five. That's okay, right?"

I nod and straighten the sheets.

"What's wrong?"

"Nothing?"

"Did I upset you?"

I curl my lip slightly and shake my head. "No, you were perfect."

"Then why do you look so sad?"

"I, uh . . . I've never had a date for them. Usually, I just stand around and watch the couples dance. Sometimes I hang out with Luna and her man du jour. But mostly, I feel really alone."

"Didn't your ex go with you?"

"No. He said it was boring. He always had an excuse for why he couldn't make it."

"Well, you're my girl now and I'll be damned if you don't have someone to dance with all night long."

I stare at the blanket as I allow his words to sink in.

He slides on his shoes and puts his wallet in his pocket. He checks his phone briefly and puts that in his pocket as well. "I have to go. Take your time. Stay as long as you want. I'll call or text tonight. Let me know when you get to work so I know you're safe."

I nod.

He kisses the top of my head and then walks out the door.

I sigh as I gaze around his room. I slip out of the bed and walk over to the bathroom sink. I lift his cologne and smell it. My knees go weak. I spray it on the T-shirt I'm wearing and decide I'm taking the shirt home with me.

As I grab my clothes off the chair, I see my book on the dresser. Sure enough, there are Post-it tabs sticking out the edges. I open my purse for a pen and flip the paper to the title page where I write, "Fisher, reality is better than fiction when I'm with you. Xoxo, Macy Greer."

A part of me wants to go through all of his things, but I decide against it. I won't be *that* girl. Instead I freshen up, put on my bra and skirt, and head home to shower. Before I leave I reach into my purse and pull out a small bottle of my perfume. I spray it on his pillow so he thinks of me. There are some things we women have to do. That was one of them.

CHAPTER 19

I straighten out my dress and stare at myself in the mirror and smile. I decided to wear the gown Fisher sent to me at the gala tonight and it's beautiful. The black sequins sparkle in the light. It's off the shoulder and makes my breasts look full and plump. The man has excellent taste. I shouldn't be surprised.

I'm just about to slip on my shoes when my phone rings. Could he be early for once? I shuffle to the phone. I don't recognize the number, but I answer anyway.

"Hello?"

"It's me. I had to borrow a phone to call you."

"I was just thinking about you."

"I'm so sorry, but I'm going to be late. We've done five takes of this scene and the director wasn't happy with the lighting, so we're doing another in fifteen minutes."

"Oh. Okay. No problem." My heart drops into my stomach.

"I'm going to be there. I promise. Don't think I'm standing you up, because I'm not."

I nod and take a deep breath to hold it together. "I understand. You have to work. It comes first."

I hear someone call his name in the background. "Okay, on my way. I have to go. I'm sorry I can't be there to pick you up. Text me the address and I'll be there as soon as I can. You save all those dances for me."

"Be careful. Good luck."

He ends the call without saying goodbye. I'm sure he was in a rush, but I can't help but wonder if he'll make it at all. I slip on my shoes, grab my handbag and keys, and walk out the door. Once I'm in the car, I text him the address. I have a pep talk with myself all the way there. I arrive at a quarter to seven and silently berate myself for always being early. I should know better. I don't want to be the first one. Ugh.

By six fifty-nine I can't stand waiting another second.

"Ms. Greer. Thank you so much for joining us. We're honored to have you as our guest tonight. Thank you again for the generous donation. We placed you and your guest at table five just across the dance floor."

She glances behind me. "You did say you had a guest?"

"Yes, he's running late with work."

"Oh certainly. Can we get you a drink?"

I shake my head and roll my eyes as I walk to my table. I've known her for years, and she and I both know I've never brought a date. I'd bet money that she's thinking I said I had a date just so I could not look pathetic. I bet she feels sorry for me. Heck, I feel sorry for me.

Reaching into my purse, I pull out my phone and text Luna.

Me: *Where are you?*

Luna: *It started at seven. Please tell me you and Mr. Smolder aren't already there?*

Me: *I'm here alone. As uz...*

Luna: *What? Okay, I'm rushing. We'll be there in a jiffy.*

I slide my phone back into my purse. This should be a blast. A man carrying a tray of champagne walks by. I take two. He frowns.

"Don't judge me," I say as he walks away. This night can't possibly get any worse.

I watch couple after couple enter the room. I start to feel uneasy, so I decide to make a trip to the restroom. It's really nice inside. There's even a couch. I sit on the couch near the door and make myself comfortable. There's no one here. Shit, I could stay here all night. I smile to myself at the idea.

I'm not sure how much time passes, but the bathroom starts bustling with activity. I sit on my couch and watch woman after woman come in to fix her makeup or spray her hair. An older woman leaves her purse on the sink as she turns to exit. I tap her on the arm when she walks by me. "Excuse me, I think you forgot something." I point to it and she gasps.

"Thank you, dear."

She whispers to her friend, "They always have such nice help."

She hands me a five as she leaves the room. That's when I decide it's time to go. I bypass the hall and head straight to my car. I'm just about to climb inside when I hear my name shouted across the lot.

"Macy! Macy, don't you dare!"

I cringe as guests eyeball me and Luna as she sprints toward me in her gown. I can see from her date's expression that he doesn't know what to think.

"What the fuck?" she huffs as she approaches. She stops and bends at the waist to catch her breath. She's holding her shoes in her hand. "Were you really leaving?"

"I don't want to do this. I don't belong here. Some lady thought I was staff and tried to tip me."

"You don't look like staff to me. Is that Fisher's dress?" she asks, eyes wide. "That man is going to bust a nut when he sees you. Is he here yet?"

"I have a feeling he's not going to show. He had to work late. There have been nights he didn't get done until two in the morning. Knowing my luck, this will be another of those nights."

"How many times have I told you about the law of attraction? Think positive, sister."

"Yeah, yeah."

A man walks up next to Luna and she leans on him as she puts on her shoes. "Tiger, Macy. Macy, Tiger."

"Tyler?" I ask for clarification.

"No, Tiger," he corrects. "Like a lion."

"Got it. You two go ahead. I'll be there in a minute."

"Oh, hell no. If I turn my back, you're going to leave. Come inside. Now."

I sigh and walk with her because she's right. I would have left. I wish this night were over.

Luna knows a lot of people. She stops every few feet and introduces me to everyone she knows. If the pronunciation of Tiger's name was a drinking game, I'd be wasted by now. I pass the time making mental note how many times he has to correct people from Tyler to Tiger. At one point he claws the air to get the point across to an older woman. She nods politely and then cringes as she struts away. I find myself actually having fun. It might be at Tiger's expense, but he doesn't seem to mind.

We sit through a slideshow presentation, speech, and a dinner. I glance at my phone several times. Still nothing from Fisher. It's after nine and deep in my soul, I know he's not coming. I feel it.

The band begins to play and couples make their way to the dance floor. "Do you mind if we dance?" Luna asks nervously.

"Gosh no. Please go for it." I smile brightly because I don't want her to feel sorry for me. As soon as she's distracted on the floor, I decide to make a run for the bathroom so I can avoid watching the dance fest for yet another year. Maybe my couch is open.

Just as I stand, I feel a tap on my shoulder. "May I have this dance?"

I spin excitedly, thinking Fisher made it after all.

"Hello, Greer."

My mouth drops and I feel like I may lose my chicken dinner. "Ollie? What are you doing here?"

He points across the dance floor to a skinny blonde in pink as she laughs with a group of men by the bar. "My girlfriend asked me to come. How could I say no?"

I cock my head to the side. Did he just say what I thought he said? "Aww, did you break up with grandma?"

"Don't call her that. And if you mean Wanda, then no, I still see her from time to time."

Wanda. What a name for a whore. He broke up our marriage over an old fish. "Does little Suzzie Q know you're playing the field?"

"Why, are you jealous?"

I roll my eyes and turn away.

"You look good. Have you lost weight?"

I sigh. "What do you want?"

"I heard about the book and movie deal. Congratulations. I always knew you'd be successful. You've always been so talented."

"How would you know? You never even read one of my books."

"That's water under the bridge now, isn't it?" He takes a step closer and rubs my bare shoulder with the tips of his fingers. "The truth is, I miss you. How about we step outside and catch up in my car?"

I'm going to spew. "Eww. No. Didn't you say you had a date?"

He glances over at her and back at me. "If we make it quick, she won't notice. Come on. Once more for old time's sake?"

"I'd rather have my head chopped off, shit poured down my neck, and my head placed on backward for the rest of my life than let you touch me one more time."

He snickers and takes my wrist in his hand as I try to walk away. "Okay, then I'll settle for a dance. You owe me that, don't you think?"

I hear him before I see him. "I'm afraid all her dances belong to me."

He's still a few feet away when he says it and I watch him strut over to me in slow motion. He's got that Kevin Bacon

"Footloose" thing going on as he crosses the dance floor in his black tuxedo and perfectly coiffed hair. I moan lightly in approval as I hum the song in my mind.

"Hey, sweetheart, sorry I'm late." He kisses me directly on the lips and pauses to stare into my eyes before he turns his attention to Oliver. "Would you like to introduce me to this douchebag who apparently thinks he has the right to touch you?"

I snicker as he holds out his hand to Oliver, who refuses to shake it back while I introduce them. "Oliver Buckner, this is Patrick Fisher. Fisher, meet my ex douchebag." Fisher recoils his hand and smirks.

"I'm sorry did you say Oliver Fucker? That's appropriate."

"*Buck-ner*," Oliver corrects angrily. "Or maybe you should just call me Greer's husband."

"You forgot the 'ex' part. You're shorter and uglier than I imagined. Huh. I'd like to say it's nice to meet you, but that would be a lie. Would you like to dance?" he asks, turning to face me.

"I'd love to."

He takes my arm and wraps it in his but turns back to Oliver before leading me away. "And for the record, if you ever touch her again, I'll break every bone in your body. Have a good night."

My lips press into a fine line to avoid laughing, but as he spins me gracefully onto the dance floor, I can't help but let it loose.

"I leave you alone for one second . . ." He smiles as he pulls me against him. The band is playing "Fly Me to the Moon," but Fisher sways with me like it's much slower, placing my hand in his against his chest. "I'm so sorry I'm late. Can you ever forgive me?"

"You were forgiven the moment I heard your voice."

He steps back and twirls me around. "Is this my dress?"

"It is. I thought I'd finally see if it fit."

"It fits. You look absolutely stunning. Oh, your surprise just arrived."

He nods off to his right and Chloe waves in the distance. I gasp and run off to hug her. "What are you doing here?" I ask.

"Fisher mentioned a gala for a good cause and I'm all about dressing up, so here I am!"

"You look beautiful!"

"So do you. Oh see, Fish, I knew this would fit her."

He shrugs. "I had no idea what size you were."

"Girl, I knew the minute I saw it that this dress was made for you. Now what was all that I missed? You looked like you were about to pounce on that creepy dude over there."

"That's my ex. He brought a date but was trying to get me to leave to have sex with him."

"What?" Fisher asks, gritting his teeth. "That deserves a punch in the mouth."

I pull him back and Chloe says, "Why don't you let me take care of him? You two have fun." She rolls her tongue around her teeth and scowls like she has a horrible taste in her mouth. Then she plasters a fake smile on her face and struts over to him.

"I don't know if that's a good idea."

"Don't worry. Chloe can take care of herself. She's probably tougher than I am."

I watch as Oliver falls all over himself to talk to her. After a few minutes he's dancing with her. Never mind that she's taller than him. She winks at us as he twirls her around the floor.

"Are you all right?" Fisher asks. "I hate that you were here all alone."

"I was for a while because I got here way too early. I was about to leave, but Luna stopped me." I motion to her and Tiger on the dance floor. She sees me and waves to Fisher. She licks her finger and touches it to her hip like it's hot.

I roll my eyes and gaze down at the floor. Fisher lifts my chin with his fingers. "I promised I'd be here. I'd never let you down."

I smile as I gaze up into his eyes. I don't know why I always doubt him. He's always come through for me. He's amazing.

"Dance with me?" he asks.

For a moment, I forget there's anyone else in the room. He leads me out to the floor and pulls me close. I lean my head on his chest and take a deep breath. He's here. I couldn't have invented a better man. I'm one lucky girl.

CHAPTER 20

After an hour of dancing, I can barely walk. I'm not used to wearing heels. The crowd is starting to dwindle down and I yawn.

"You look like you're ready to go."

"Is that okay?"

"I'm ready when you are. Let me say goodbye to Chloe." We scan the room for her. Fisher points to her at the bar. She's talking to Oliver's date. It looks heated.

"Uh-oh."

Just when we think hair might be pulled, they hug it out instead. Then Chloe leans forward and whispers something in her ear. She covers her mouth, laughs, and nods. Chloe leans on the bar as Oliver's date stomps over to him. She's yelling at him and pointing to Chloe. Chloe waves. Then she picks up Oliver's drink and tosses it in his face.

Fisher slaps his knees and laughs.

She says one more thing to Oliver and he turns pale. She walks back over to Chloe and high fives her before she struts out of the room. Oliver chases after her, flicking Chloe off as he runs.

"Shall we go say goodbye now?" Fisher asks.

"Definitely."

She smiles as we approach. "You sure do know how to keep things interesting."

"Oh, Fish, you know I don't play."

"What happened?" I ask.

"Let's just say I let Oliver feel me up a little. Then I let his girl know what happened. She was really pissed when I told her he asked me to go out to his car for a quick one."

I cover my eyes in embarrassment. I can't believe I was married to that.

"She said she appreciated me telling her. Then I whispered that I was a transgender but still had a penis." She shrugs. "I enjoy watching assholes get what they deserve. Are you getting ready to go?"

"Yeah, I'm tired. I hate wearing heels. I'm not very good at being girly."

"Hey," Luna says, rushing over. "You leaving?" she asks.

"Yeah, I'm beat."

She winks at me and I roll my eyes but grin at the same time.

"Chloe, you're not leaving yet, are you?"

"Hell no, girl. Let's dance."

They take off to the dance floor waving goodbye to us. The lights are down low and the band is clearing out. They're playing current hits, and Chloe and Luna are the only two dancing. I didn't even know they'd met.

Fisher holds out his hand to me and loosens his tie. I stumble walk a few steps. "Take them off if they hurt."

He doesn't have to tell me twice. I remove my shoes and sigh in relief. He picks them up and carries them to my car.

"I hate that we didn't drive together. Will you call me when you get home?" he asks.

"Oh. Do you work tomorrow?"

"No."

"Oh." I pick through my purse like I can't find my keys. I don't know how to do this.

"Why do you ask?"

I shrug. "I wondered if maybe there was a chance you'd want to maybe . . . come over?" I gaze up at him through my eyelashes, almost afraid to hear him say no.

He takes a step closer to me. "You want me to come over?"

I sigh. Why does he have to make this so hard? "That's what I said, didn't I?"

He smirks. "I didn't know if I heard you right. It's late. What would we do once we got there?" He pushes a strand of hair behind my ear.

"I thought we could play Monopoly. What do you think?"

He laughs and pulls me to his chest. "You're really sweet, you know that?"

"Sweet? Wow, thanks. I think I like drunk Fisher better. Drunk Fisher said I was hot."

"Oh really? Is there something wrong with being sweet?"

I shrug. He leans his forehead into mine. "I bet you taste sweet."

I swallow hard. Oh Lord. What if I taste like stale Cheerios? "There's something you should know."

"Okay." He pulls away to look into my eyes.

"You know the douchebag? Well . . . he's the only guy

I've . . . Ugh."

"What? Are you serious?"

I open my car door and toss my shoes and purse on the seat. I slam the door and lean against it. "I'm sorry."

"You're sorry? Why would you be sorry for that?"

"Because I don't want you to be disappointed that I'm not the experienced woman I seem to be in my books. Truth is, I've never done half that stuff."

Fisher looks around the lot and watches people getting into their cars and limos. "Why don't we go back to your place and talk about it there? I don't think this is the place to have this conversation."

I nod and open my car door.

"I'll follow you, okay?"

"Sure."

It's a twenty-minute drive back to my apartment. The entire drive, I regret saying anything to him at all. I should have just slept with him and not said a word. Maybe I wouldn't have been bad and he would've never known.

I park my car and Fisher parks next to me. I lift my shoes and my purse and open my door, prepared to apologize for saying anything.

He struts purposefully around the car, his tie hanging loose around his neck.

"Hey, can we just forget I said—"

I don't get a chance to finish my sentence before his mouth is on mine. He bends down and lifts me into his arms and carries me into the building. He puts me down when we step in the elevator, pushes the button for my floor, and then presses himself against me into the elevator wall.

"Do you think I care what you have and haven't done?"

His breath is heavy as he trails the back of his fingers down my cheek. "All I care about is all the things I'm *going* to do to you. Tonight."

The door pings and opens.

I stand frozen. He's so fricking hot. He takes a step forward. The doors almost close, leaving me inside. He puts his hand in between the doors and snickers.

"Don't chicken out now. I promise I'll be gentle, unless you want me to be rough."

I gulp. He holds out his hand to me and smiles. "Come on."

He leads me to my door and takes my key. Unlocking my door, he places his arm on the frame and watches me walk inside. He closes the door behind him and locks it.

"Give me your phone."

I reach into my purse and hand it to him. "Why?"

"I just want to make sure you didn't send any emergency texts to Luna tonight."

I can't help but grin. "You don't want to be interrupted?"

He shakes his head. "Should I barricade the door? Does she have a key?"

"I don't think she'll be bothering us. Um . . . do you want to watch TV?"

"No."

"Do you want something to drink?"

"Do you?"

"Yeah. I could use a drink." I drop my purse and shoes on the floor and take off to the kitchen. I remove the plug from my half-empty bottle of wine and pour myself a full glass. "Did you want one?"

"Are you nervous?" he asks.

"Me? No." I grab at my throat and open my mouth widely. "I'm just parched." I turn and chug the glass of wine.

"We don't have to do anything, you know. I'd be perfectly fine watching a movie and rubbing your sore feet."

"Really?" I ask.

He nods and smiles. "I'd wait forever for you."

His words hit me in the heart. They're perfect in every way. It's like he stepped out of the pages of my mind.

I gaze at the small patch of fine hair that's peeking out from his open shirt. I look into his big brown eyes and see the peanut butter streaks of gold. His lips are wet and there's a small shadow of hair across his cheeks. It makes him look even sexier than before. I don't want to be afraid anymore.

I stare at the floor as I confess. "I want you. I've always wanted you."

"Greer, look at me," he whispers.

Raising my eyes to meet his, I notice he seems worried. "What is it?"

"I need to tell you something. I've wanted to say this to you for a while, but it never felt like the right time."

Oh no. He's married. He's got a girlfriend back home. I bear down and prepare for the worst.

"This thing we have going on here is special. You're important to me. And while I'm insanely attracted to you, I need you to know this isn't me just being a guy. This isn't me just wanting to fuck you."

"Do you? Want to fuck me?" I ask biting my lip.

"No. I don't. Well, yes, I do. But first I want to make love to you. Then I'm going to fuck you."

I moan lightly. "That's what you wanted to tell me?"

"No. You need to stop distracting me with your pouty,

plump, kissable lips and words about fucking. My dick is already hard."

He shakes his head and takes a deep breath as I giggle at his comment.

"This is serious."

I nod playfully.

"I'm serious."

His face loses all trace of humor and I stiffen.

"What I wanted to tell you . . . what I need you to know before we take our relationship to the next level . . . What I want you to know is I love you. I'm *in love* with you."

I gasp. Grabbing his face in my hands, I search his eyes. "Really? Are you sure? Because you don't have to say that just to get me to sleep with you. I'm going to sleep with you tonight whether you love me or not."

"Do you not believe me?" He half laughs, semi concerned.

"I don't want you to say it because you think it's what I want to hear. I want you to say it because you're sure. And . . . I want you to love me, but I don't know how you could. I mean, have you looked in the mirror lately?" I walk around him and turn.

"I don't understand."

"You're hot, Fisher. Smoking hot. You're a damn model, for fuck's sake. You scream sex. I only pretend. I write it."

"Baby, don't you see how amazing you are? I know the fucker hurt you. Luna told me all about him. I hate that he's made you see yourself in such an undeserving light."

I shrug. "When you hear it for long enough you start to believe it."

"Then I guess I'm going to have to tell you how fucking gorgeous you are until you believe that too. Do you know what you do to me, woman?"

I shrug and he shakes his head.

"You don't see the way men stare when you walk into a room. You are every man's wet dream and I speak from experience."

"Whatever." I sigh and close my eyes.

"Look at me."

I do as I'm told.

"I love you."

I squeeze my eyes shut, tears building behind my closed lids.

"You are amazing and funny and kind. You're sweet and stubborn. Sassy and silly. You challenge me. You make me laugh. You make me want to be good enough for you. I want to make you happy. I want to give you everything because I love you. Do you hear me?" he asks, pulling me by the waist.

I cover my eyes with my free hand.

"I love you and yes, I'm damn sure of it. I wouldn't say it if I didn't mean it."

I shake my head. He pulls my hand away from my face and holds it against his heart. "I. Love. You." He whispers the words in my ear and they slowly fill every cell of my being. You know that scene from "Breaking Dawn, Part Two" where the venom takes over Bella's cells and fixes all her broken pieces? Yeah. That's how I feel. I feel like he's stitching up my pieces and making me whole.

I lean my forehead against his and he wipes a tear away from my cheek. Then he kisses it softly. "Patrick?"

"Uh-oh. You never call me that."

"I'm calling you Patrick because it's your name and I want you to know I'm being serious too."

"Okay . . ."

Taking a deep breath, I admit my feelings to myself and him in three, well, four, little words that pack a punch. "I love you, too."

His lip curls up on the side and he kisses me tenderly.

"Now that we got that business out of the way, what was that you said earlier about wanting me?"

"Hmm . . . I kinda feel like playing Monopoly now."

"No, you don't."

I lick my lips and lean back against the counter, taking him in like he's water and I'm a sponge.

"What?" he asks.

"Come closer."

As he steps into me I pull his tie out from around his neck. He watches me.

I slip my hands inside his tux coat and over his broad shoulders, sliding his coat off his arms and onto the floor.

Raising my hand to his face, I touch his lips with my index finger. He closes his eyes as I trail my finger down his chin and his neck. Once I reach his collar, I tug on the buttons, pushing them through their tiny holes. The act in itself is turning me on.

He inhales deeply and watches me button for button. My desire builds with every single one. As I reach the last button before his belt, I tug his shirt free. He leans forward, encasing me between him and the counter.

I hurry to set him free, pushing his shirt off his shoulders and exposing his perfect chest. I gaze up at his eyes for a brief moment and bend my head to kiss the area just below his ear. I position my lips around his earlobe and give him a little preview of what it feels like to have my lips sucking a part of him.

He moves in closer to me and places his hands on my back. My dress loosens as he carefully unzips me. Goose bumps break out all over my arms.

Kissing and licking his neck, I take in his perfect scent. The one that drives me wild.

My dress falls to the floor, leaving me standing in a strapless bra and underwear.

His hand reaches behind me and grips my ass. "Still want to play?"

I shake my head as he lifts me onto the counter. He greedily kisses my neck and cups my tit in his hand, tugging at the material to expose my breast. The cool air makes me inhale quickly. It doesn't take him long to kiss his way down my chest. He takes my nipple into his mouth, licking and sucking it so perfectly, I almost feel like I could orgasm from that alone.

Placing his hands on my thighs, he kisses my breasts. His hands move to the top of my thighs and his thumbs rub the outside of my underwear. I wonder if he can tell how wet I am.

He steps back and pulls my underwear down my thighs and drops them on the floor. He spreads my legs and kneels on the floor in front of me, kissing the inside of my thighs all the way up to my pussy. I moan as his lips and tongue taste and devour me. Sliding my ass forward to the edge, I lean back to give him better access.

I stare at my ceiling as my hands grab ahold of the back of his head.

He eats me like he's starving and the passion he has for it makes me spiral out of control. Before, it was waves on the beach. This time, it's electrical shocks shooting through my veins. I cry out in pleasure as he pushes his finger inside me.

My writing will never be the same again. I never knew it could feel like this. Holy shit, am I going to come again? Boom. The lightning hits, causing me to buck my waist. Bam! Another ripple of pleasure shoots through me all the way to my toes. I must be dead. This can't be real.

He kisses his way up to my stomach and smiles, his face wet with me. He pulls me off the counter and carries me to my bedroom, placing me on the bed before he removes his belt. Reaching behind me, I undo the clasp of my bra and toss it on the floor. Then, I help him with his pants.

He tugs at the buttons on his wrists and removes his shirt. I pull on his belt loops, causing him to take a step toward me. I slowly unzip his zipper and slide his pants down his legs. He runs his fingers through my hair and hums lightly. He steps out of his pants and removes his socks. I pull him closer once more. Sticking my tongue against his belly button, I lick his muscled abs. I play with the waistband of his boxers before I run my tongue along the edge.

Gripping his back with my hands, I slide them down every muscular curve and arch until I reach his boxers. I slowly tug them down until he's naked in front of me.

My memories didn't do him justice. I grip his dick at the base and run my tongue along his shaft. He moans.

Licking the edge along his head, I take him in my mouth. I didn't really enjoy this before him, but the way he's responding, along with the way he tastes, makes me think I'd be happy to do this every single day. I love it. I love the way he feels in my mouth. I love the way his hand grips my hair. I love the way he gazes down into my eyes and watches my mouth around his cock. I love it all.

As my desire grows so does my speed.

"Stop, before I cum." He pushes my head back softly and I attempt to go back for more. He laughs. "If I cum now I'll have to wait a while before I go inside you and I can't wait."

He bends down and takes a condom out of his wallet. I crawl backward on the bed until I feel my pillow. I lie down and he crawls over me.

"Do you want me?" he asks.

"Yes."

"Tell me what you want, Greer. Do you want it soft or hard?"

"Yes. I want it all."

He smirks as he slides the condom over his length and hovers above me, rubbing his cock on my thigh.

"You're such a tease," I say as I attempt to reposition my hips so he's closer to entering me.

He kisses me as he slowly pushes inside me. He's way bigger than I'm used to and I feel every single inch of him. I love sex. Sex is the best thing that was ever invented. Thank God he gave men dicks. Dicks are the best thing in the world.

He pushes in and out of me, going deeper with every thrust. He's sweating as he bends down and bites my bottom lip. I grab ahold of the back of his neck and pull him into me. Our tongues invade each other's mouths as he picks up speed and power. I feel him touch my core and holy shit. It feels amazing.

I lift my legs higher and he plunges deeper. "Oh yes. Yes. Oh my God, yeah," I shout. His breaths come quicker as he stills and shakes, falling on top of me, still inside me. Our connection is undeniable. He is more than I ever dreamed and he's all mine. I thank the universe and swear to think positive forevermore.

CHAPTER 21

I wake to the smell of bacon, which is surprising because I know my fridge was empty. I'm deliciously sore as I pull on my robe and freshen up in the bathroom. When I arrive in the kitchen, he's standing in his boxers at my stove cracking eggs.

"Good morning," I say, leaning on the wall.

"Hungry?"

I bite my lip and gaze at his gorgeous body. "Uh-huh."

He smirks and flips a piece of bacon. I walk behind him and kiss his back, sliding my arms around to the front of his chest. "Where did you get all this? I know I didn't have any food."

"I ran out while you were sleeping."

"In your boxers?"

"No, I got dressed and then I got undressed again."

"Oh, why is that?"

"Because I hoped you'd look at me the way you are and that maybe we'd have a little something before breakfast."

I chuckle into his back. "I think that could be arranged. So you cook, huh?"

"I dabble."

"It smells really good."

He turns off the heat on the stove and slides the eggs to the back burner. He turns to face me and bends to kiss me. "How are you feeling this morning?"

"Like I had amazing sex last night."

"Hmm. I had amazing sex last night, too."

He kisses my neck and I hear a buzzing sound coming from the table. He turns to look in the direction of my cell. "It's been doing that all morning. I'd bet money Luna wants a full report."

He starts plating the eggs as I walk over to the table and read my messages.

"Congrats, you won. But . . . oh, wow. She said I need to check my email. The script is done. They want to start casting."

I rush to my laptop and sit on the couch. I open the file and read it out loud. "They've scheduled a first round casting call for Wednesday in L.A. I guess I'll be flying out Wednesday morning."

"That's great news. How exciting."

He places the plate in front of me on the coffee table and hands me a napkin and a fork.

I push my laptop away and start eating. "So good. Thank you so much. You always feed me."

"I learned early that your stomach is the first step to your heart."

"Well, you have my heart, remember?"

"How could I forget?"

"When do you work next?"

"Tomorrow. Do you believe this is my last week?"

"What?" I drop my fork on my plate and wipe my face with my napkin. "Then what?"

He shrugs as he takes a bite of bacon. "I guess I'll need to talk to my agent. She usually has something lined up. Maybe a commercial or a modeling gig."

"But then you'll have to leave. Right?"

"Stop. I know what you're thinking. It's going to be fine. As it is, we spend a lot of time on the phone already. I'll just be a little farther away."

I place my plate back on the table and cross my arms.

"You didn't finish."

"I'm not hungry anymore. I don't want you to leave."

He leans over and kisses my cheek. "It'll be fine. You're going to be swamped with the movie. I'll fly back to visit and you can visit me. Who knows, maybe my next job will be here. Let's not panic until I figure it out."

He's funny. Not panic. Ha. I've already run multiple scenarios in my mind, all of which involve him on the other side of the world. I stare at my laptop. I don't want him to go. I've gotten so used to him being around that I took it for granted. How can I get him to stay?

My eyes focus on the word "casting call." Instead of a lightbulb over my head, I see fireworks. Brilliant, perfect fireworks. I grab ahold of his arm.

"Fisher, you're Penn."

He laughs. "Thanks. I figured that out a long time ago, but it's nice to hear you admit it."

"No, I mean you could be Penn."

"I could be, huh?" He places his plate on the table and

leans over me, pushing me into the couch. "Does that mean you'd like to take on a different chapter? Isn't there a shower scene?"

He kisses my neck and starts to untie my robe.

I push his chest. "No! I mean you could try out for the role of Penn. Come with me to L.A. You fit him to a T because you *are* him. Oh my God, Fisher. Think of it! We could work together."

I expect to see his face light up with excitement, but he frowns instead. "No. I don't think so."

"What? Why?" His head drops and I slide out from under him. "What the fuck?"

"I just don't think it's a good idea. We're together and I like things how they are."

"So you like the idea of leaving me then?"

"That's not what I said."

"Then why won't you try?"

"I don't want to get the part because I'm dating you. And besides, would you really want to watch me be Penn with a Kasey that isn't you?"

I ponder those words. That would suck. "I guess I'd have to be an adult, wouldn't I? If it meant you stayed here, then it would be worth it."

He shakes his head as he picks up our plates and walks back into the kitchen.

"I can't believe you're saying no!" I yell, following him. "What's the real reason? Are you trying to get away from me?"

His brows furrow. "You can't be serious."

"What would you think? Huh? What would you think if I had the chance to stay with you, do what I love to do, and accept a life-changing career opportunity, but instead I said no? If I said, no, Fish, I'd rather fly halfway around the world to pose for a crappy magazine layout than spend months in your bed."

"That's not what I meant and you know it."

"Then why not? I'm telling you I want you to do it. To at least try."

He leans forward, placing his elbows in the counter. He scrubs his hands over his face. He almost seems worried.

"I mean, you might not even get it. Maybe they'll think your acting sucks and you don't look like Penn at all."

His head quickly turns to regard me and I press my lips together to avoid laughing.

"You think I don't look like Penn?" he asks, taking a step toward me.

I back up and shrug. "I mean, Penn was a risk taker. You don't really act like him either."

"I don't?" he says, puckering his lips like he's getting mad.

"Nah. You're right. Why bother. You probably wouldn't get it anyway."

He steps toward me again more quickly and I run back to the bedroom screaming.

He chases me and I start laughing. I stop at the foot of the bed and he slowly stalks over to me like a predator.

"Now, Fisher," I say, raising my finger to him. "You need to behave yourself." He keeps walking forward, eyes dark. I drop my robe to the ground and stand naked in front of him. He stops briefly and greedily devours me with his eyes. He slides his boxers down his legs and I bite my lip.

He strides over to me and turns me around so I'm facing

the bed. He kisses my neck and reaches around me to caress my breasts. I feel his erection against my ass. As he bends me forward, I absolutely know he's way better than Penn could ever be. He will stay with me. One way or another, I'll make this work.

CHAPTER 22

" "Thanks for coming here to see me on such short notice, Fabian. I know we fly out tomorrow, but I really need to run something by you."

"I'm all for hearing your ideas. What's this about?"

I turn my laptop around and show him multiple pictures of Fisher. "What do you think of him?"

Fabian leans forward in his seat and pulls my laptop closer to his face. "He's attractive. Good jawline. Great body. I'd do him. Why?"

"Can you keep a secret?"

He nods. "I can try."

"What if I told you he was my muse? What if I told you I modeled the book after meeting him on the beach in Florida and that the first three chapters were absolutely real?"

His face lights up.

"And what if I told you he was a talented up-and-coming actor who's due to arrive here to pick me up in a few minutes?"

"I'd inquire as to whether or not you're asking me to do a casting call right here?"

"Is that bad?" I wring my hands and cringe.

"Does he have something prepared? I mean, it's not completely my decision. He'd have to meet with the head of casting and the director. Assuming we liked him, we'd have to see if he had chemistry with our Kasey."

I nod. "The thing is, he doesn't really know he's coming in to meet you. He thinks we're going to dinner."

Fabian sits back in his chair and opens his mouth to say something, hesitates, opens his mouth again, and abruptly closes it.

"Is it the worst idea you've ever heard?"

My phone buzzes. "Yes, Brenna?"

"Patrick Fisher is here for you."

"Okay, give me a minute."

I grit my teeth as I stare at Fabian and wait for a response. He adjusts the glasses on his face. "Well, don't keep the man waiting. Bring him in."

I clap and rush over to the door. Brenna is rubbing her stomach as she smiles at Fisher. His face is pale. He looks like he might pass out. "Everything okay?" I ask.

He trudges toward me and takes my hand, pulling me into my office. He doesn't notice Fabian, who's moved to the back wall to look at my book collection. He closes the door.

"You're pregnant?" His eyes are dark. He's pissed.

"What? No? Who told you that?" As the words leave my mouth I recall Brenna rubbing her belly and shake my head.

"Why did your assistant just congratulate me then? We've had sex, like . . ." He counts on his fingers. "Six times, in two days. You couldn't possibly be already!"

I gaze behind him at Fabian, who motions for me to keep going.

"This is all a big misunderstanding."

"Oh really? Because I'm starting to feel really pissed off right now, Greer. Are you pregnant? You said it had been forever since you'd been with anyone. And only your stupid ex. Was that a lie?"

This is embarrassing. Oh shit. Fabian's recording us on his phone. The things I do for love.

"Listen to me. The other day, or a week or two ago, I don't remember . . . I was thinking about you and how you gave me butterflies. My stomach was flip-flopping around and it made me happy. I touched my stomach and told the butterflies I loved them and I wanted them to stay. Brenna walked in on me. I felt like an idiot, but . . . when she asked I figured she was joking. I didn't know she really believed it!"

He steps back and seems to think for a moment. "You have *butterflies* in your stomach?"

I nod.

"Not a baby that isn't mine?"

"No. And not yours *yet*, anyway."

He smiles and places his hand on my waist. "I give you butterflies?" He's doing that smoldering thing again and I forget Fabian is in the room.

"Every time I see you, think of you, or touch you."

"So you have them now?"

"Uh-huh."

"Have I told you yet today how much I love you?" He lowers his head to mine and kisses the top of my head.

"And cut!" Fabian shouts from behind us.

"What the fuck?" Fisher yells, spinning around.

"That was fabulous. Just fantastic."

Fisher does a double take at Fabian, then glares at me.

"Patrick Fisher, let me introduce myself. My name is Fabian Confey and I'm on the casting team for *Book Boyfriend*. Can I just tell you that your pictures don't do you justice? If I asked you to walk back in and repeat that word for word with the same intensity, could you do it?"

He glares at me. "Did you set me up?"

"Don't be mad. I just wanted you to meet him. I didn't know all that was going to happen."

"Who's your agent? Do you have a portfolio? Are you coming with us to L.A. tomorrow?"

"Can you excuse us for a moment?"

Fabian nods and gives me the thumbs-up as he leaves my office.

Fisher inhales deeply and crosses his arms.

"He likes you," I say nervously.

"Did you not hear me when I said I didn't want to try out for the role?"

"I heard you. I just didn't listen. How many times did I tell you to stop trying to be Penn? Did you listen? No! And now that I want you to be Penn you won't even try. Do you have any idea how frustrating that is?"

His face softens.

"Is it awful that I want the man I love to stay in town? Is it bad that I've watched every single commercial and scene you've ever been in on YouTube and that I think you're incredibly talented? Is it awful that I think my movie would be lucky to have you and that I know women around the globe will love you just as much as I do?"

He brushes a stray hair out of my mouth and tucks it behind my ear. "I guess it could be worse."

"If you really and truly hate the idea of being Penn then I'll tell Fabian to forget it."

He gazes at the ceiling. "Does it mean that much to you?"

I nod.

"Then how can I possibly say no?"

I jump into his arms and he laughs.

Deep in my soul, I know everything is going to be just fine.

Falling back onto my bed in my hotel room, I contemplate taking a long nap. Whoever invented 5:00 a.m. flights should be shot. At least I don't have to be downstairs for casting for three hours.

My phone pings with a text.

Unknown: *Hey, girl, it's Chloe. I hope you don't mind my texting you. I was chatting with Fish and he told me you were in my neck of the woods. What time do you get in?*

I create a contact for her.

Me: *Just got to my hotel room and of course I don't mind. We should have exchanged numbers sooner.*

Chloe: *Where are you staying?*

Me: *JW Marriott*

Chloe: *No shit. I'm literally down the street. How*

about I walk over and we grab coffee?

Me: *Sure. I'll meet you in the lobby.*

There goes my nap but oh well. Maybe coffee will help me perk up. I brush out my hair, slip on my shoes, and take the elevator to the lobby. She's already there.

"Hey, girl, hey!"

We hug and she points to a coffee bar in the hotel.

"Perfect," I say.

I get a pumpkin latte and she gets black coffee with sugar.

"So how have you been? Did you like the gala?" I ask.

"Loved it. I've been fine. I started this new job as a receptionist and it blows. Not all of us get regular gigs like Fish."

"Did he tell you I want him to try out for Penn?"

She waves the air as she sips her coffee. "I've been telling him that since the day I heard it was going to be a movie."

I smile and blow on my cup. It's too hot to drink.

"Can I just tell you I still fangirl every time I hear your name? I've read every single one of your books."

"You mentioned that." I snicker. "Really, I'm just a normal person who got lucky."

"Fish is the one who got lucky. When he told me he literally ran into you when he was in Florida, I about died."

I laugh. "Yeah, I guess it was even funnier when he found out who I was."

"He knew the moment he saw you. I talked about you all the time. I tried to get him to read *Weeping* once. I remember he looked at your picture and said you were cute. Funny how things work out, isn't it?"

She shakes her head and I feel as if I heard her wrong. I replay her words in my head. "When did he tell you he met me?" I ask for clarification.

"He called me the next day before he went on set. He said, 'I ran into your favorite author yesterday on the beach.' I think he followed it up with you being even prettier in person." She winks at me and laughs as my heart sinks.

"So he knew I was an author the minute he saw me, huh?"

"Oh absolutely. Poor guy heard me talk about you every time a new book came out."

I stare down at my coffee cup and move it around in my hands to warm me. My blood is suddenly cold.

"When I heard you were making a movie, I told him he should look you up and try out for the part. He finally picked up the book and read it. I only asked him like ten times. I've never seen him read a book so intently. When he found out that first part was him, oh Lord, you'd think he won the casting lottery!"

I swallow hard and jump from my seat.

"You okay?" Chloe asks. "What's wrong?"

"I, uh, I just remembered I was supposed to check in with the director and start reviewing stuff. I'm sorry to cut this short. I have to go."

I practically run from her without saying goodbye. Hitting the elevator button repeatedly, I pray it opens before I burst into tears in the lobby. He knew it was me? He lied to me. Oh my God. He is an incredible actor. He had me completely fooled. I've been played from day one.

CHAPTER 23

I've ignored all his texts and messages for the past two days. I've written angry letters to him to figure out exactly what I'm going to say. I've gone over every detail of our entire relationship. It's been one complicated plot after another.

Luna called me three times today. I can't talk. I somehow managed to get through auditions and only broke down once. I texted Luna to let her know I was fine. She said Fisher was freaking out and wanted me to call him.

I bet he's freaking out. I wonder If Chloe told him about our conversation. I don't blame her. She obviously didn't realize what he was doing or she wouldn't have said anything.

I haven't been able to sleep. I was supposed to fly home yesterday, but I canceled my flight. I told Luna I needed a break and I'd be home soon. She begged me to call her, but I just can't. How do I tell her how badly I fucked up this time?

I knew it was too good to be true. There's no way he'd ever love someone like me. I should have known better. After

Ollie left me I was desperate to feel wanted by someone. Knowing he cheated on me for years with an older woman who was ugly as fuck was a blow to my ego. Didn't I give him everything I had? It wasn't enough.

Enter perfect Patrick Fisher. Momma always said, if something seems too good to be true, then it probably is. Or maybe that was Oprah. Regardless, I ignored all my instincts because deep down I wanted a happily ever after. I should know better. There's no such thing. There's a reason they call them book boyfriends. It's because they only exist on paper. They aren't real.

There's a knock on my door. Wow, that was fast. I ordered a bottle of wine five minutes ago.

I pull a five out of my wallet and open the door to Fisher. I try to slam the door shut, but he pushes his way inside.

"What the fuck, Greer? Do you know how worried I've been? Why won't you answer my calls?"

"Get out!" I yell, pointing at the door.

"What's going on? Why are you so angry with me?"

I walk over to him with the full intention of slapping him in the face, but he grabs my hand mid-air. "For fuck's sake, baby, talk to me."

I pull my hand out of his grip. "Have you spoken to Chloe?"

"Yeah, why?"

"Did she tell you then?"

"She told me you were talking about the movie, you freaked out, and ran off without saying goodbye. She said you didn't answer any of her texts either. Did she say something to upset you?"

I huff and pace as the tears flow down my cheeks.

"What's going on?" He rushes over to me and tries to pull me into a hug. For a moment, I consider letting him, feeling his arms around me one more time. But then I feel sick. Sick with his lies and his games, so I push him away. "You lied to me!"

His eyebrows furrow.

"You told me you didn't know who I was when we met in Florida, but you knew exactly who I was, didn't you?"

His face is etched with concern. "Is that what this is about?"

"Answer me! Did you know my name?"

He sighs. "Yes, but—"

"And the reason you read my book was because Chloe told you they were making a movie and you saw your in, right?"

"That's not exactly true . . . I—"

"And you thought if you showed me you could be Penn, I would fall for you, and maybe even give you the role, right?"

"Okay, wait a minute. I told you I didn't want anything to do with it. You forced me into considering it."

I shake my index finger at him repeatedly as I pace. "Oh, you're good. You're an even better actor than I ever dreamed."

"Greer, let me explain!"

"That's *Macy* to you!"

He almost seems like he's going to cry.

"Wow! Crying on demand for a part? That's pure talent, folks. Pure talent."

"Can you let me explain?"

"Have at it. Let's see if your improv skills are any good."

He shakes his head. "Yes. I did know who you were when I looked down and saw I'd knocked you over. I didn't knock you down on purpose if that's what you're thinking."

I turn my back to him and gaze out the window, wiping a tear from my cheek.

"I didn't know what to say. I was worried you were hurt. Everything after that was one hundred percent real, I swear."

"Even the part where you asked me my name like you didn't know it?"

"Okay. That wasn't exactly real. I did know who you were, but then you gave me your real name and I figured you didn't want me to know you were an author. I went with it."

"You went with a lot of things."

"I fell hard for you that night. You were smart and funny. Distant and different. I saw something in your eyes."

I spin around to face him. "You saw an easy target. Someone who'd been hurt before and was easy prey for a man like you."

"No."

"If you were so enamored with me and you knew who I was, then why didn't you call me? Why not call me and tell me you fell for me? Oh, that's right. Because I didn't have a movie role for you yet."

"Dammit! Stop creating a story where there isn't one. I called that number because I wanted another shot with you. When I realized you gave me a fake one, my heart sank. I figured a woman like you was used to having guys like me around. I assumed you only wanted that one night and nothing more."

I roll my eyes and sit on the couch. He walks forward and sits on the coffee table across from me. He tries to touch me and I pull away.

"Chloe talked about reading your books for years. I told

her I saw you, but that was it. I never told her anything about what happened between us. It was mine and mine alone."

"How chivalrous to not kiss and tell."

"Will you stop? Let me finish. She kept pushing me to read *Book Boyfriend* and when she mentioned it was becoming a movie, yeah, I'll admit, it made me interested. But I was in the airport just like I told you when I saw it. I flipped it open and read the first few pages. When I read what you wrote . . . When I realized it was me? Shit, Greer. You have no idea how happy it made me. It made me think I was more than just a night on the beach. That maybe you felt something, too. So I bought the book and read it twice. Then I started reading your other books. It took me a while to try to think how to contact you. When I saw what you made me, Penn, out to be, I was worried I'd disappoint you. So I tried to be who you wanted."

I stare at the carpet. I refuse to look at him.

"You have to know, it was never about the part. It was always about you. I love you." He reaches out to touch my cheek and I push his hand away, jumping to my feet.

"Stop! Just stop! Why not tell me this from the start? Why lie?"

"I told you what I thought—"

"What you thought I wanted to hear."

"No! I told you what I thought would make me look better. You already thought I was a crazy stalker. I didn't want you to know I was already in love with you from the first page."

The tears flow down my cheeks. "You knew I'd been hurt before."

"Yes."

"And you knew how hard it was for me to trust anyone,

much less you."

He nods and scrubs his hands over his face.

"Yet you lied anyway."

"I never wanted to hurt you."

"But you did. I trusted you. I loved you."

He stands and walks over to me. "Don't say loved as if it's past tense. This was a misunderstanding. That's all. It doesn't change a thing."

"No, Fisher. That's where you're wrong. It changes *everything*."

CHAPTER 24

Dog videos aren't doing it for me anymore and that's saying a lot. They were my go-to for happiness and now I don't even have them anymore.

There's nothing left to distract me from my thoughts. It's been a week since I came home. One hundred sixty-eight hours and forty-three minutes since I broke up with Fisher.

He hasn't tried to call me. I asked for space and he's given it to me.

I know Luna's worried about me and the circles under my eyes. I don't sleep and I don't eat. What I do is miss him terribly. I sleep with his stupid shirt and cry all the time. I replay all his words over and over in my head. I want to believe him, but I'm scared that it isn't real. That he isn't real.

I live in a world of fiction. My world consists of make-believe stories where good triumphs evil and love always wins. But we all know, good doesn't always win. Turn on the TV and watch the news. Evil exists. Bad people do bad things and get away with it every single day. People with big hearts try to make up for all the sadness in the world by giving themselves away and then you hear they were murdered while helping a homeless person or stabbed when they gave their lover one more chance. Love doesn't win. Love scars.

Books have always been my escape. I can leave my life behind and get lost in someone else's. I can fall in love with a man covered in perfect words and actions. These books are not only my life, they're also my income.

I know for a fact there are millions of people like me in the world. People who want to believe love—true love—is real. That there are still good men out there somewhere, waiting to be found. Honest men who don't cheat or lie, searching for us like we're searching for them.

But then you open your heart. For one moment, you let someone in even though every single part of you is screaming to protect yourself. You don't listen because the hope for something greater is better than the reality that you're alone and always will be.

They say time heals all wounds, but all it does is numb the pain. You never heal from a broken heart. You learn to live with whatever you have left. You make it work the best you can. That's what I'm doing. At this point I'd kill to be numb.

"Sorry to bother you, but Fabian is here. He seems irritated. Luna asked me to get you. She wants you in her office. Her exact word was, 'Now!'"

Brenna seems afraid. I bolt out of my chair and rush into Luna's office. Fabian is pacing.

"What's going on?"

"You! I blame you," he says, pointing at me.

"What happened?"

Luna sighs.

"We loved him. Even though we've never done this before, I had the director watch my recording. The chief of casting called and spent an hour with him on Facetime. We found the ideal actress to play Kasey and they look perfect together. Today we offer him the role and he flat out turns us down! Turns *us* down! I thought you said he was a shoe in?"

I glance at Luna and she shrugs. "Fisher turned it down? Why?"

"He said he never wanted it to begin with. Now we have to start over. We had our hearts set on him."

Fabian turns to face me. "You need to come to the office tomorrow and meet with the director. I'm sending you a bunch of headshots and videos. Go through them and help me find a backup. I haven't told him yet. I want to have an alternative we can sell before I open my mouth."

"I'll go look right now. Fabian, I'm so sorry. This didn't work out for any of us."

Somberly, I trudge back into my office. He turned it down? It's exactly what he wanted. Why would he do that?

As I walk to my desk, I notice a small box sitting in the center. It's addressed to me. "Brenna? What's this?"

"Oh sorry, that came for you while you were in your meeting." She does jazz hands. "Mail day!"

She's sweet and I know she has the best intentions, but she obviously doesn't realize that no one can make me smile right now. Even the cast of SNL with guest star Eddie Murphy would have their work cut out for them.

I slide into my seat and stare at the box. It's small and square. There's no return address and the label is typed. Slicing the side with my scissors, I toss them back in my drawer and pry the box open.

Before I can look inside, Luna knocks lightly on the open door. "Got a second?"

I place the box on the floor by my feet as she walks in.

"I'm really sorry. I didn't mean to fuck this up. Fabian was really pissed. I'm sure you are too."

She ambles over to my desk and sits on the corner, staring at me. She's oddly quiet.

She takes a deep breath after what seems like forever. "Here's the thing. I know we'll be able to find another actor. I'm not worried about Fabian. I'm worried about you."

"Me? Why? I'm fine."

"Are you?"

As I gaze up into her eyes, I remember how well she knows me and my already weak wall starts to crumble. I stare down at my hands. "I don't know what I am."

"We've known each other a long time. I was there when you met and married Oliver. I was there to see you happy, sad, and everything in between. The fact is, I never liked Oliver. I thought he was an ass from the start."

I sigh. "I know. We've had this conversation a million times."

"What I'm trying to say is that I consider myself a fairly good judge of character. I've been with a lot of men in my life and I feel as if my bullshit radar is superb."

I lean back in my chair and run my fingers through my tangled hair. "What are you trying to say?"

"You're a mess, Greer."

"Wow. Thanks. See, I've known that for a while."

She rolls her eyes. "That's not what I mean. I know you miss him and it's eating you up inside."

My bottom lip trembles and I clear my throat to keep the

tears at bay. I shuffle some papers around on my desk.

"He screwed up. I get that. But you know what? I liked him immediately. I didn't get a single bad vibe from him. Not one. My meter never went off. Believe me when I say I watched for a reason not to trust him. He was almost too good to be true."

"He wasn't true, Luna. That's the point. He lied. They all lie."

"No one is perfect and to be honest I was relieved when he screwed up."

Did I hear her correctly? I laugh sarcastically. "I'm glad it made you happy."

"Hear me out. Fisher said and did everything just right for too long. Sure he can't sing or play piano, he's not *that* perfect, but he was damn near close. Tell me you weren't waiting for the ball to burst?"

I gaze up at her intently. She has my attention.

"In the grand scheme of mistakes, this wasn't the worst. And his explanation made sense. I think he was telling the truth. I don't think this was about the movie at all. I think it's always been about you."

"You don't know that."

"I know *you*. I know that it's easier for you to believe it was all a lie then to believe the man really loves you. All those years I watched you fight for a morsel of love and compassion from Oliver. And those morsels were few and far between. When you got them you gobbled them up like a five course meal, but they were never enough. Then here comes a man who sees just how amazing you are and instead of accepting the meal, you're still waiting to starve."

I stand and cross my arms, walking to the window. "I

don't know what you want me to say here. I'm hurt that he lied. I gave him my heart and he used it for a movie role."

Luna shakes her head. "Do you really and truly believe that's all it was?"

I shrug.

"I'm not trying to tell you what to do. But I've never seen you happier then I have these last few months. And I'm sorry, but I saw the way he looked at you when no one was watching. Men don't fake that shit unless they have an audience."

I cover my face with my hands and Luna wraps her arms around me.

"No matter what you decide, I'm here for you. I just had to get that off my chest because I love you."

"I love you too, Luna."

We both wipe our eyes and Luna coughs lightly. "Alright, friend time is over. Back to work."

She trudges out of my office without saying another word. Emotions are hard for her. I'm really blessed to have her in my life. Even though I know she meant well, his lies are still echoing in my head. I don't know how to get past them or if I ever can. Although, she made a point I hadn't considered.

Was I waiting for him to mess up so I could run? I want to say it's the dumbest thing I've ever heard, but knowing my track record, she could be right. I think back to all the times I expected him to disappoint me. I was scared he'd hurt me and I was anticipating it every time I saw him. That wasn't fair to him and yet he never wavered. I do miss him. Should I have given him another chance?

As I sit back down in my chair, my foot kicks the box and it rattles. I'd completely forgotten about it. I wipe my eyes and lift it onto my desk.

There's lots of bubble packaging. As I unwrap it, I see a taco menu folded around something. I don't know why tacos and Fisher go hand in hand. I think I just have him on the brain. Inside the menu is a Ziploc bag full of shells. I gasp. The menu is from Florida. My heart constricts as I read the note.

Greer,

I know you're done with me and I can't say I blame you. I screwed up. Nothing ruins trust faster than lies, even lies made with the best intentions. I was wrong and I'll regret it for the rest of my life.

I wanted you to know I meant what I said. Meeting you on that beach was one of the best things that has ever happened to me. I saved the shells you asked me to put in my pocket that night. I was going to make something out of them for you, but, well, we both know that isn't going to happen now.

Take care of yourself. If you ever need me, I'll always be there.

Fisher

The taco menu is from where we ate that night. He kept that too? What kind of guy holds onto seashells for months? I know the answer to that; a sensitive, caring one. A guy who might have actually wanted to remember me. Did he? Was he telling me the truth?

Leaning back in my chair, doubt invades my mind once more. Maybe I gave up too soon. He turned down the role. Why did he do that?

I have questions and I need answers. I pick up my phone and call the only person I trust to tell me for sure.

"Hello?"

"Chloe? It's Macy. Do you have a second to talk?"

"A second. What do *you* want?" Her voice is cold. She's not the same person I remember. Is she angry with me?

"I was wondering if you could tell me . . . I mean, I was wondering if you knew . . ." I don't know what I want to say.

"Listen, if you're calling to bitch me out for hiding what you think is some deep dark secret then you're barking up the wrong stripper pole. I have nothing to say to you."

"You're mad at me?"

"Hell yes, I am. You broke his heart, you bitch!"

I'm shocked. This is not the way I envisioned this conversation. "He lied to me, Chloe! What was I supposed to do?"

"You were supposed to let him explain himself to you and accept the fact he has flaws. That he makes mistakes. He's human, Ms. Macy Greer. We're not all infallible like you. He's not some perfect guy you wrote in a book. He's a guy who does dumb things but also really great, amazing things too. He's the best person I've ever known in my life and for you to hurt him that way . . . I'm burning all your books!"

She hangs up on me and I stare at my phone. I immediately redial her number. She won't answer. Holy shit!

I broke his heart? I remember his face when I told him I was done. I remember when I thought he might cry and I made fun of him. I know I was angry, but I was also *really* mean.

Is he okay? I've been sitting here licking my wounds and never once considered he was hurt too. Could he really have faked all those intimate moments with me? If it was all for a role, why did he turn it down?

I try to call Chloe once more and there's still no answer. I text her.

Me: *I fucked up. I'm going to call him. I'm sorry.*

I stare at Fisher's number for a second and think what I'm going to say. My phone rings and startles me. It's Chloe.

"Hello?"

"If you really want to apologize to him you're going to have to hurry."

"What do you mean?"

"He's on his way to the airport. He's going home."

"Home? Like to Cleveland?"

"Yes, he's flying Southwest, flight 2082. It leaves in an hour out of San Fran. Run, Macy. Go get him!"

"Thanks, Chloe. I'm so sorry."

"Girl, stop apologizing. Go. I'll forgive you when you fix him!"

I grab my purse and sprint out the door.

"Macy? Is everything okay?" Brenna asks.

"With any luck, it will be soon."

CHAPTER 25

Driving while trying to book a flight on your Southwest app is a really bad idea. Parking your car and not caring where isn't good either.

I run through the airport like a bat out of hell. I just need to make his flight. That's all I ask. I have thirty minutes to get through security and get to the gate. Thank God I have TSA Pre-check.

I stand in a short line that seems to be taking longer than the long line next to it. When I finally get to the conveyor, I place my purse on the track and watch it get sucked through the X-ray machine. I step through the people checker. No alarms. Yes!

I wait for my bag and it doesn't come out.

I tap my foot as a guard walks over to the attendant at the machine. They chat for way too long. Is he telling her about his weekend? He lifts my purse. "This yours?"

"Yes, is there a problem?"

He snaps gloves on his hands and pulls up the image on a

separate screen. "What would that be right there?"

"Oh shit. I mean sorry. It's my perfume."

"It needs to be in an approved quart size bag. Is it less than three ounces?"

"I have no idea."

He reaches in and slowly pulls it. I feel my heart racing. How far is the gate? Am I going to make it?

"Keep it. Or throw it away. I'm really late. Can I please go?"

"This is expensive stuff. My wife wanted it and I said hell no. Unless Walmart carries it, she ain't getting it."

"Take it. Give it to her with my blessing. But please, will you let me go through?" I beg. "There's this guy and I love him and he's about to get on a plane and I don't want him to leave without me."

He sighs. "You sure?"

I nod.

"All right. I'll keep it. Go."

I gaze down at my ticket. "Where's Gate 28?"

"Ooh," he says. "What time is that flight?"

"Thirty minutes. Umm . . . I glance at the clock on his computer. It's in ten minutes!"

"It's all the way down that corridor to your right. You'll be lucky to make it if you run."

My shoulders slump. Maybe this is fate telling me to quit. Maybe I'm not meant to stop him. I want to cry. Maybe if I call him . . .

"How's your foot?" he asks.

"My what?"

"That foot. Didn't I see you limping?" He winks.

"Umm. Yes?"

"Pedro!" he speaks into his microphone. "Where you at?"

"Security."

"I got a priority woman with a bad foot who needs a fast ride to 28. You got it?"

The tires squeal as a cart stops in front of me.

"Thank you so much . . ." I pause to get his name.

"Nelson. Go get your boy!"

I jump on the back of the cart and hold on for dear life as Pedro drives in and out of people, honking his horn the entire way. Nelson was right, I would've never made it. As we get closer to the gate, I see the back of Fisher's head as he boards the plane. They close the doors behind him.

"No!" I yell. "Wait!"

I take off running, trying to pull my ticket up on my phone at the same time. I get to the gate and the gentleman shakes his head. "I'm sorry, ma'am. Once those doors are closed, I can't open 'em."

"But, there's a man on that flight I really need to talk to. Please?" I beg.

"I'm sorry. No can do. If you step over to the desk, we can help get you on a different flight to Cleveland."

"I needed to be on that flight," I say in a whimper. I walk over to glass and stare at the plane as it backs away.

I lean my head against the window. "I should have just called him," I say to no one.

"What would you have said?"

I spin around so quickly, I almost lose my balance. Fisher is standing before my eyes, bag in hand.

I jump into him and throw my arms around his neck, sobbing.

He pats my back lightly, but it's different than ever before. He isn't holding me. He's trying to be nice. Have I lost him forever?

"You're still here. Why? I thought I saw you get on the plane."

"The bigger question is why are you here, Macy?"

He called me Macy. That's not good.

"I got the shells."

"Oh." He resituates his backpack on his arm and glances out the window.

"You kept them."

"Yes. But now they're yours."

I stare at his beautiful face. He looks tired. His face is stubbled as if he hasn't shaved in a while. He makes very brief eye contact with me and then looks away, sighing. "Do you have something you want to say? I need to catch another flight."

"Don't go," I blurt out the words the second he talks about leaving.

"Why would I stay? There's nothing keeping me here."

"I'm here."

"You're not mine."

His words and the matter-of-fact way he says them feel like a blade slicing through my chest. "I'm so sorry, Fisher. Can you ever forgive me?"

His eyebrows furrow and he studies my face.

"I've been absolutely miserable. I cry constantly and I miss you. I know you tried to explain things to me and I didn't listen. But I was angry and scared. I've been lied to before. I know you're different. I know you weren't trying to hurt me, but at the time, it felt all too familiar."

His face is stone. I'm not getting through to him at all.

"From the start, I never believed a guy like you would ever even look at a girl like me. Then slowly, you made me feel like I was enough. You made me feel like we belonged together. Then you . . . and when I . . ." I choke back the words. I can't get them out.

He gazes at the ceiling and takes a deep breath.

I sniff away the tears and notice a group of people watching us, including Pedro on his cart. "Pedro, please. Go help some other pour soul! And to the rest of you gapers there's nothing to see here. Move it along. Mind your own fucking business," I shout.

I rub my nose with the back of my hand and briefly glance up at Fisher's face. He's smiling. "You have such a way with people."

I cock my head to the side as a tear rolls down my cheek. "The only person I want to have my way with is you."

He reaches out and wipes the tear away with his thumb. "You hurt me."

My chest heaves. I manage a nod.

"And I hurt you."

I nod once more.

"How about if we agree to never do that again?"

"Really?"

He holds his hand out to me. "Is it a deal?"

"Are we shaking on it?" I ask.

"Don't people usually hold their hand out and say deal when they expect a hand shake?"

"I guess."

"Well? Are you going to leave my hand out here hanging? Are you refusing my offer?"

I stare up into his eyes and he seems to read my thoughts.

"I swear to you on my life that this was never about the movie. You had my heart the second I landed on top of you on that beach. You've always had it and you always will."

I place my hand in his and he pulls me forward until I crash into his chest.

"Is that a yes?"

I grip his beautiful face in my hands and smile.

"Let's make it official." He lowers his mouth to mine and I throw my arms around his neck. It's the best, most important kiss of my life.

There are cheers and applause all around us. We both grin.

"Show's over, folks," he announces.

"It was never a show," I reply. "It was real."

He kisses the top of my head and breathes me in. I grasp his arms as questions burn in my mind. There are things I need to know. "Can I ask you something?"

He steps back to see my face. "Oh boy, your nose is twitching. Maybe we should sit down." He leads me to some chairs and he drops his backpack on the floor. "Ask away."

"Why didn't you get on the plane?"

"Chloe called me. She said there was a chance you might be coming to try to stop me."

"And you waited?"

"I watched the last person boarding. They asked me if I was coming and I couldn't do it. Knowing you wanted to talk to me was enough reason for me to stay. I would've stayed here even if you didn't show. Just on the off chance you might call."

My heart aches. "You seemed so angry and cold. I didn't think I was going to get through to you."

"I'm sorry. I wasn't exactly sure why you wanted to see me. I was afraid it was only about the film."

"Why did you turn it down?" I ask, touching his arm.

"That news traveled fast. The only reason I ever considered it was because of you. Without you in my life, I could never even pretend to be Penn. It would hurt too much."

I pick the lint off my shirt and flick it to the floor. "You scared me when I found out you lied. I was worried it was the beginning of the end. The start of a long string of deception."

"I was wrong. I promise you I'll never lie to you again. Ever."

I gaze up at him through the tops of my eyelashes. "Even if I ask you if my butt looks fat?"

He smirks. "Even then."

I sigh and yawn.

"You look exhausted."

"I haven't slept much."

"Me neither."

"I don't even remember where I parked my car." I laugh and scratch my head.

"That's pretty bad. I think you win. I see you didn't pack much."

"I didn't pack anything."

"What would you have done if I *was* on that flight?"

"I would have taken the next one."

"Whoa, that's some serious stalking. Should I be concerned?"

I crawl over my seat and onto his lap. "Yes. I'm your fan now. I missed you."

"I missed you, too."

"I'm sorry."

"You already said that," he replies, brushing my hair out of my eyes.

"You didn't seem like you believed me. You called me Macy." I grip my heart.

"You told me to call you that."

"I didn't mean it."

"I know."

"Are you still going to Cleveland?"

"My mom is expecting me, but I don't think I could leave you tonight if I tried. Do you know anyone who might be willing to give me a ride and a place to stay for the night?"

I slowly raise my hand. "Assuming we can find my car."

"If we found each other through this mess, your car should be a piece of cake."

He leans forward and places his forehead against mine. He closes his eyes and releases a deep breath. I couldn't have said it better myself.

CHAPTER 26

Did I actually wake up before him? I softly kiss his chest as I lift up on my forearms to see his face. He's sleeping peacefully, and I can't help but stare. I roll over and look at the clock. It's almost nine.

"Shit!" I jump out of bed and run to the bathroom naked. I'm supposed to meet Fabian at ten and it's a forty-minute drive. I'm never late! Never!

I run back and forth between the bathroom and the closet, pulling on a new pair of underwear, putting toothpaste on my brush, stuffing it in my mouth, and clasping my bra.

I glance at the bed as I rush past and Fisher is up on his elbows watching me. He has a ridiculous smile on his face.

"It's not funny! I'm late!"

"I wasn't laughing. I was admiring."

I spit my toothpaste in the sink and rush into the closet. Yoga pants for a movie meeting? No. Fuck! What do I wear? I grab a pair of dress pants and sit on the edge of the bed, praying I can zip them. They slide on perfectly. I guess being too sad to eat has its perks.

"Your tits look amazing when you run."

I roll my eyes at him but silently cheer that anything looks good on me naked.

Heading back into the closet, I grab a blouse and rush back to the bathroom. Where's my dry shampoo? God bless the person who invented it.

Fisher leans on the bathroom door completely naked and crosses his arms. I stare at his reflection in the mirror and bite my lip.

"Don't rush. You'll be fine."

"You don't understand. I was supposed to look through videos and pictures last night to find a new Penn and I completely forgot. Fabian wants to tell his boss we found a replacement for—" I stop and turn to face him.

"What?"

I drop my hairbrush in the sink and take his hands.

"What's going on?"

"How much do you love me?"

He grins. "I thought we covered that last night. Do you want me to show you again?"

"Would you do me a really big favor?" I pull his hands against my breasts.

He glances down. "Absolutely."

"Be Penn."

"No."

"Fisher, please!"

"Greer, we discussed this the last time you brought it up. From the day I read that first page that job meant nothing to me. I'm not going to risk losing you again."

"You won't. Please?"

"I love you and I'd do anything for you. But I won't do that."

I try to avoid singing Meatloaf's "Paradise by the Dashboard Light," but it's no use. It's in my head now. "Fabian was so angry with me. They loved you. They wanted you so bad their mouths were salivating. Fabian hasn't told the director yet because I was supposed to find Penn last night. I did find him. At the airport."

He rubs his face with his hands and walks back into the bedroom, bending over to get his boxers.

"Do you have another job lined up?"

He pulls them on and sits on the bed. "Not yet."

I get down on my knees in front of him.

"Greer, stand up. Don't do that."

"Patrick Fisher, I made a huge mistake. I assumed all men were alike and I was wrong. You're not like other men. The truth is you're better than any man I could have ever written. All other book boyfriends I try to write and all book boyfriends I try to read will forever fail to compare to what I get to kiss at the end of the night."

He huffs out my name. "Greer . . ."

"I always thought this was a fantasy: the butterflies, the phone sex, the dates that end with sweet kisses, and the guy who always seems to say exactly what I want to hear, until I met you."

"Greer!"

"Shh. Let me finish. You stepped out of a book and showed me reality was better than fiction. You're the real deal, Fisher. And there's no other man in the world who could be Penn. There's no other man like him because he's based off of you. I used to say he *was* you, but that's not true. He has nothing on you, you're way better."

"Can I say something?"

"No. Wait. You would slay this part. You'd be amazing. Hell, I'll even tell the world I wrote the book off of one night with you. Then I'll spend the rest of my life beating off women with a stick. Just please think about it. Don't say no."

"Are you finished?" he asks.

"Yes." I lower my head, defeated.

"I tried to say yes the minute you got on your knees, but you wouldn't let me. Don't ever get on your knees in front of me again unless we're being intimate. You should never, ever have to beg me to give you anything. Everything I have is yours, including my heart."

"Really?" I jump up and tackle him on the bed. "You'll do it?"

"If it's what you want and you're sure it will never come between us."

"It's what I want." I kiss his face repeatedly. "Thank you, thank you, thank you!"

He laughs as he spins me around so I'm underneath him. "Just promise me that if anything is bothering you, you'll tell me. And there will never be any need to beat anyone with a stick. I only want you."

I lift my head and kiss his lips. I try to deepen the kiss, but he breaks it. "I guess I'd better get dressed. Looks like I'm coming with you."

I gaze into his eyes and see my love for him reflected back at me. "You're definitely coming, but I think I'm okay with being a little late after all."

He presses his lips to mine and all is right with the world. Maybe the law of attraction is true after all. I wrote an amazing man and the world one upped me. I can live with that.

Time doesn't heal *all* wounds. But Patrick Fisher is the best Band-Aid I could have ever hoped for.

Book boyfriends are fun, but *real* men are even better.

The End

EPILOGUE

One year later

Fisher

"Babe, are you almost ready?" I glance at my phone. We walk the red carpet in a little over an hour. Luna and Fabian want us there early for pictures.

"Give me a minute. You're lucky. You have no idea how hard it is to do hair and makeup."

"Oh I don't know about that. I've sat in many a chair being made camera worthy. But you don't need any of that. You look your hottest first thing in the morning if you ask me."

"Yeah, well. I think you're biased. I don't need pictures plastered all over the globe of People Magazine's Sexiest Man Alive and his frumpy, just rolled out of bed girlfriend."

"I'm sorry, but who almost punched a reporter for commenting on your tight ass just last week?"

"You." She rounds the corner and my heart almost beats

out of my chest, I grab ahold of it to keep it inside. "Holy fuck, Greer. You're a vision."

She twirls around in a floor-length red dress that makes her sexy skin radiate even more. "Goddamn."

"You're too good to me. And that suit?" She fans herself. "I'm going to peel that off of you with my teeth tonight."

"I'm going to hold you to that. But right now, we need to go."

Marcus is waiting for us outside the door of the penthouse suite where we're staying in L.A. I nod to him as we exit, and he holds the elevator door.

When we first asked him to help us out during filming, he gave me major attitude. But now that we've spent some time together, I think he knows I'd do anything for Greer and he respects that.

Filming went off smoothly and the production house worked their asses off to get the premiere timed for the release of the final installment of Greer's trilogy. It was originally supposed to be just one movie, but when the second book was an even bigger hit than the first, they signed us up for all three. Her final book comes out next week and she won't be able to stop me from reading it when it's finally on the shelves.

She said she wanted me to be surprised and that it had to be perfect. She should know by now that I think she walks on water. I'd read her chicken scratch on a napkin and love it. She's the most talented woman I've ever known.

When we get to the lobby, we're joined by additional security. Marcus ushers us off to a room for pictures. Luna and Fabian are inside.

"Excited?" Fabian asks as he shakes my hand.

"Nervous."

"You have no reason to be. Early reviews are coming in and they're off the charts."

"What's a woman gotta do to get a little attention around here?"

I turn in time to see Chloe make her grand entrance. She rushes over to Greer and hugs her before me. I'm okay that they talk more than we do now. It's important to me that my two best girls get along.

"I'm not one to usually go for blondes, or women for that matter, but there's something about her. Wow. Will you introduce me?" Fabian asks.

"Absolutely. Chloe, this is Fabian."

"Well, hello there, handsome. Come here often?"

"I'd come here all the time if you were here."

Chloe laughs and winks at me as Fabian ushers her toward the bar.

"Hey." I feel a nudge and know who it is without looking.

"Hey yourself, moon girl."

Luna leans her head on my shoulder as we watch Greer get her picture taken. "I feel like my baby is all grown up."

I smile. "You did an amazing job with her."

"Right? I'd make a great mom. I just need a sperm donor."

"Did I ever say thank you to you for speaking to her on my behalf?"

"Only like twenty times. But just so you know I'm still watching you. I always will be."

"I'm counting on it."

I feel another head on my opposite shoulder and it's oddly familiar. "Oh, Patty, you're such a manly man. Can I get your autograph?"

I shake my head and push my younger brother with my hand. "Hey, asshole. Who invited you?"

"Your hot girlfriend. By the way, does she have a sister?"

Luna clears her throat. "Hi, I don't believe we've met. I'm Luna, Greer's twin."

I watch as he takes her hand and kisses her knuckles. "I'm Paul, hotter brother of the sexiest dickhead alive. Can I buy you a drink?"

"Drinks are free," she replies.

"In that case, I'll buy you two."

I roll my eyes as they walk off to the bar. Fabian rushes over to me. "Hey, just in case you forgot, after this movie tour is over you have two weeks until filming starts again."

"I'm going to need that time. I have a book to bring to life."

"What? Does Macy know what you're up to?"

I grin and shake my head. "What fun would that be?"

"I swear you two could have a movie based on your movie. Did you read the third one yet?"

"No, she won't let me."

"Hold on." I watch as Fabian scrolls through his phone. "I just sent you the pre-release I got. But if she asks, you didn't get it from me."

I nod and pat him on the shoulder. I open my email and there it is. The sequel to Book Fiancé is Book Husband. I'm relieved to know she keeps me around. I skim the first few chapters and stop when I get to the wedding.

"Hey, gorgeous," Greer yells. "Come get your picture taken with me."

I stroll over to her and kiss her on the cheek. She looks at me with so much love and adoration that I feel the need to thank my lucky stars once again.

I lean over and whisper in her ear as the cameras flash. "So now do you believe in fate?"

She smiles. "Yes, I do. I also believe in tacos. Can we get dinner after this?"

I smile. "Two steak and one chicken."

"And guacamole."

"Only if you wear a tomato in your hair."

"Why not! It matches my dress."

"Fisher, over here, please."

We turn and realign our bodies in the direction of the loudest photographer.

"What were you and Fabian talking about?" she mumbles through a smile.

"Oh nothing."

"Hmm. I don't believe you."

"You'll find out soon enough."

As the camera flashes again, I wrap my arm around her and smile to myself. She wrote an amazing sequel and I plan on making every one of her dreams come true. If a proposal and husband is what she wants, a proposal and husband is what she gets.

Penn Fitzgerald will strike again.

Acknowledgements

There are so many people I need to thank. I hope I remember everyone. Let me start off by saying thank you to all my friends and family who have supported me on my never-ending journey.

To my father, Dave. Dad, I don't know if you know what's been going on with me all these years or not. I like to think you're watching over me and the boys and that you know what's in my heart. Thank you for teaching me to dream and to want more. I will always be a Chiletz through and through and I hope our family name continues on through my books long after I'm gone. I love and miss you daddy.

To my mom, Diane. I miss you every single day. Thank you for showing me how to be strong and how to continue on when things are at their worst. There are still days I reach for the phone and wish I could hear your voice one more time. I love you.

To my boys, Tyler and Ryan. This has been a rough year for us, but I want you to know how proud I am of you for staying brave and strong when things get tough. I couldn't have gotten through this without you. You will always be my true loves. You are my heart and soul.

To Kim Hurschik. I don't even know what more I can say that you don't already know. You're my person. Thank you for listening and always encouraging me. Your faith in me and my potential has seen me through more days than I can count. I'll love you forever, sister.

To Dorrie Cortesi. Thank you for helping me try new things and for getting me better than most. I'm blessed to have you in my life and I will always be there for you no matter what. We've got this. Love you, girl.

To Cheri Rubocki. Even though you hated me for being a goody two shoes growing up (LOL—for a little while anyway) you are still one of my dearest and oldest friends. Thank you for listening without judgement, for laughing at my stupid jokes, and for always making me feel that I'm not as crazy as I think I am. You have been an amazing support to me this last year and I want you to know how much I admire and love you.

To Brenna Leigh. How can I put this into words? I know I've told you all this before, but I hope you truly know how much you mean to me. You are beautiful inside and out and I thank God that we found each other. Thank you for being the fastest reader/ proofreader in history and for always being will-ing to tell me the truth. Even though I gave you a hard time about it, it was exactly what I wanted and needed to hear. Thank you for being my friend. And Brenna is not like you in any way other than the fact that she has an amazing heart. I flove you.

To Misty Marcum. Misty. Misty. Misty. Misty. Look fa-miliar? Thank you for finally answering my texts after I write your name a hundred times. You have one of the most beauti-ful and kindest souls I've ever known. Thank you for texts, messages, and phone calls whenever I need you. Thank you for always believing in me no matter what. I love you. Don't ever forget that, even when I'm a pain in the ass.

To Jennifer Mock. Knowing you are reading my words always makes me anxious because your opinion means so much more to me than most. Thank you for supporting me and being my friend. You are a bright light in my world, my friend. Love you tons.

To Hazel James. Thank you for always being my sounding board and my friend. Thank you for cheering me on when I have no cheers left to give. I'm grateful to have you in my life.

To Andee Michelle. Thank you for our four-hour phone calls and for listening to all my thoughts and fears. You are one of the most beautiful people I've ever known, and your friendship means more to me than all the tacos in the world. #SoulSister.

To Murphy Rae. Even though I'm old enough to be your older sister (ahem), you never cease to amaze me with your insight and knowledge. You're an old soul. It's hard to believe this is our ninth book together. Thank you for always being there to answer my questions, lend support, and work with me on personal and professional goals. You're an amazing designer and an even better friend.

To Julie (JT Formatting). Even though we don't always talk as much as I'd like, I think we both know that our friendship never wavers. I believe in you. You're talented, kind, and deserving of all the good things life has to offer. Thank you for always being my friend and for doing amazing things with the crap I send you. <3

To the Twisted Chick-Lits. My team. My people. You all are my heart. Thank you reading my words and for your neverending enthusiasm. You are some of the best people I've ever known in my life and I'm glad to call you my friends.

To my laptop. If you could stop being so damn slow that would be great. Thank you for not losing my files. I'm counting on you.

To everyone who reads my stories. Thank you for reading

my words and getting my heart. I put a little piece of my soul into every single book and it still blows my mind that you take the time to pick it up. Thank you for believing in me.

Love come in all shapes and sizes with all kinds of hearts. It can best be found within yourself, first and foremost. I am a constant work in progress. We all are. Nothing and no one is ever perfect, but never stop believing or striving for better. We all deserve a happily ever after.

About the Author

Dawn L. Chiletz resides in Illinois with her two amazing boys and three loving dogs. When she's not binge writing or reading, you'll most likely find her somewhere on social media making a sarcastic comment or watching animal reunion stories while she cries like a baby.

To find out more information,
including her upcoming signings,
please visit her website at:

http://www.dawnlchiletz.com

Facebook:
http://www.facebook.com/dawnlchiletz

Facebook Reader group:
Dawn's Twisted Chick-Lits

Instagram:
https://instagram.com/DawnLChiletz

Twitter:
https://twitter.com/DawnLChiletz

BookBub:
https://www.bookbub.com/authors/dawn-l-chiletz

Other Titles by Dawn

The Contest Series:
The Contest
Waiting to Lose

Reality TV Novels:
The Fabulist
The Praetorian

Standalone Novels:
Enough
Can't You See
Confessions of a Carpool Captive
Angry Annie